Second Chance
in Asheville
A Sweet Romance Novella

Julie Milo

Cover Design by Purpose on Paper.

ISBN: 979-8-9919471-3-8

For western North Carolina, and everyone else impacted by Hurricane Helene.

Author's Note

On September 27, 2024, the remnants of Hurricane Helene steamrolled over western North Carolina in the United States. This after wreaking havoc along the Gulf coast of Florida, making landfall in the Big Bend region of Florida, and downgrading to a tropical storm over central Georgia more than five hours after landfall. The heavy rain Helene dumped on Georgia, South Carolina, Virginia, Tennessee, and North Carolina caused deadly flooding, most notably in western North Carolina, including Asheville, a popular tourist destination in the Appalachian Mountains.

Though I live in Florida along the Gulf coast, my husband and I were in Asheville, North Carolina when Helene stomped through. We were supposed to be enjoying a romantic getaway for our fifteenth wedding anniversary that we'd had planned for months. We spent Thursday, September 26 driving up to North Carolina from Florida, mostly in the rain. We knew about the weather, of course; we had just spent the last several days watching the storm to see whether it was heading our way. But between the land weakening the storm and the mountains breaking it up (Asheville is five hundred miles from where Helene made landfall after all), we anticipated a rainy Friday and then back to our scheduled vacation the rest of the weekend. Even the Biltmore Estate, when they emailed and called to cancel our Friday reservations due to "severe weather," expected to reopen on Saturday.

Of course, that's not what happened. Helene retained her strength farther inland than is typical for similar storms. The torrential rain proved too much for the mountain infrastructure and caused devastating flooding and mudslides, knocking out electricity, water, and cell service, and making all the major highways in and out of the area impassable for almost two days.

When my husband and I were finally able to find a safe route out of Asheville on Sunday, September 29, we drove until we crossed into Florida, and stopped at a hotel for the night to shower and reset before making the rest of the drive home. It was not a restful night of sleep, but the basic premise of what would become this novella came to me. At the time, I had already finished writing my debut novel, *Love in the Stacks*, and had started writing the next book in my Delaneys in Love series. However, I put Delaneys in Love book two on hold and focused on Ramona and Kevin's story of reconnecting amidst disaster. *Second Chance in Asheville* is not a romantic comedy, for obvious reasons, but I tried to make the love story the central focus, so it is *not* primarily a heavy story about a natural disaster. Writing it has been a way for me to process my emotions around the stressful and scary experience my husband and I had in Asheville.

Of course, the people who live and work in that region were far more impacted than I was with my two days of inconvenience. They are forced to rebuild their lives.

The experience that the characters in this story have on the ground in their part of Asheville during and after the storm is based on what my husband and I experienced. The timeline of losing utilities and gaining them back was the actual timing for people in Asheville. Like Ramona and her friends, my husband and I were fortunate to be staying in a family-owned vacation rental with hosts on-site and willing to share food, bottled water, information, and generator-provided electricity with us.

At the time of this publication in March 2025, western North Carolina is still recovering. If you'd like to contribute money to help with those efforts, the city of Asheville recommends donating to North Carolina Voluntary Organizations Active in Disaster members (https://www.ncvoad.org/members/) and the state government of North Carolina recommends donating to the North Carolina Community Foundation (https://www.nccommunityfo undation.org/nonprofits/disaster-relief-fund/).

Readers, be aware that this book does contain discussions of the devastation in the region, but also of the awe-inspiring resilience of a community. The story contains minimal "Biblical" swearing (four instances) and brief "Level 3" intimacy per the Closed Door Romance guidelines, but no taking of the Lord's name in vain, no sex, no cheating, and no character deaths.

Chapter One

Ramona

I f I must turn thirty, at least I'll be saying goodbye to my twenties with a bang. An autumn birthday adventure in Asheville, North Carolina with my two best friends, Katie and Beth.

We drove up from Atlanta this morning, and now we're pulling into a gravel driveway on a rural mountain road. The wooden sign at the entrance reads "King Farms." I step out of the car and am immediately greeted by the most beautiful view I've ever seen—rolling fields with a horse corral in the distance and mountainous hills beyond, still green despite the late September date.

Katie squeals behind me as she gets out of the car. "Beth, this is so perfect! A mountain getaway is just what we need."

I turn to see Beth rolling her eyes. "Why do you need a getaway?" she asks. "Are things too perfect with your dreamy fiancé?"

"Wedding planning is a lot! Don't tell me you've forgotten. It's only been five years since your wedding."

"Yeah, five years filled with pregnancy and diapers and no sleep," Beth retorts.

My two best friends are both blissfully well-prepared for the marriage and career phases of life. Beth married her college sweetheart and is the mom of two adorable babies—four-year-old Finn and two-year-old Emma—all while rocking her job as the best physician's assistant in Atlanta (though I might be biased). Katie's long-term boyfriend proposed earlier this year, and they're in the throes of planning their New Year's Eve wedding, timed so they can sneak in a honeymoon cruise before Katie has to return for the new semester at the high school where she teaches English.

Then there's me: perpetually single and constantly overlooked for promotions at the marketing firm where I work. A sigh escapes me. I'm honestly not even sure I still enjoy my job or find any fulfillment in it.

I shake my head. *No work or pathetic-dating-life thoughts this week*, I remind myself firmly. My friends and I are here to celebrate my birthday and soak up all the fall vibes of the North Carolina mountains.

I take a deep breath of the mountain air. It's cooler here, a good five degrees below what we left in Atlanta just this morning. Thank goodness. The summer was hot, and temperatures are still hovering around ninety degrees, even though the first official day of fall was yesterday.

"Let's check out this cottage," Beth trills with a clap of her hands.

We funnel toward the little house as Beth studies her phone. She flips up the cover on the electronic keypad mounted to the door and enters a series of numbers. With a beep, the lock disengages, and Beth pushes open the door.

The inside of the cottage is completely charming. We enter a small sitting area with a loveseat, a TV, and a unique coffee table made from a piece of natural wood lacquered to a shine. Next to the sitting area is a kitchenette with a small dining table. We wander down a hallway off the kitchen that leads to two bedrooms with a Jack-and-Jill bathroom in between. The decor throughout is homey and functional, with small touches that tie together the city and mountains.

"It's Ramona's birthday, so she gets her own room," Beth announces. "Katie and I will share."

"Works for me!" I smile and leave my purse in the bedroom with a queen-sized bed. Back in the hallway, I duck my head into the second bedroom, which has two twin beds. Katie and Beth are squabbling playfully about who gets which bed.

We make several trips out to the car to bring in our suitcases and bags of road snacks. It's already late afternoon, and our only plans for tonight are to go out for dinner and drinks.

Katie insists we get dressed up before we go out. She's already offered to be our designated driver, so we go along with it, not that we're planning on getting too wild.

I decide to wear the burgundy midi-dress I packed. It has cap sleeves and a deep V-neck. The bodice is fitted, and the skirt is a softly gathered chiffon with a scalloped lace hem. It's the perfect fall cocktail dress.

I sashay dramatically into the living room. Katie wolf whistles, while Beth, ever the mom, takes one look at my bare arms and says, "It's chilly outside. Why don't you borrow my denim jacket?"

I try it on, and Katie nods her approval. "Looks perfect, more 'mountain' than 'city.' You'll fit right in with the Asheville locals now."

Putting aside the debatable accuracy of her judgment of mountain chic, fitting in with the locals is apparently something Katie feels is more important for me than for herself. Her classic black swing dress has three quarter length sleeves and a belt around her waist. The bright red ballet flats on her feet add a pop of color, but don't exactly scream "mountain adventure."

For her part, Beth is giving off major nature vibes in a dark green chiffon jumpsuit with wide, flowy legs and a high neck. The green reminds me of the ridges I saw in the distance when I first stepped out of the car after we got here.

We pile into the car and drive to a bookstore in north Asheville that serves charcuterie and champagne among the shelves. Despite being a Monday night, a small crowd mills around inside and on the patio. We find a table and order a meat and cheese board, along with glasses of champagne for Beth and me, and a Coke for Katie.

As my friends chat with each other, I survey the room. As long as I can remember, I've had a curiosity about people. I see them and wonder about their lives—what motivates them, what fascinates them, who they love. I'm obsessed with the *Humans of New York* project and how it looks beyond someone's outside appearance, digging into their humanity and reminding us that everyone has successes and struggles we may know nothing about. Sometimes I play a people-watching game in my head, inventing backstories for the strangers around me. Not even Beth or Katie know about this quirk.

I watch a woman sitting alone at the bar. Her gold dress reminds me of the one Andie Anderson wears in the movie *How to Lose a Guy in 10 Days*, so I imagine she's just had an argument with her lover. Maybe they were at a fancy event down the street and she stormed out, her broken heart taking refuge here among the books. She's angry and hurt, but part of her hopes he'll come find her, which is why she keeps stealing glances at the door.

The server sets the charcuterie board on the table in front of us, shaking me from my imagination. I paste on a smile and zero back in on my friends' conversation.

"I hope Jonah's mother is nice," Beth says to Katie. "My mother-in-law is the worst. Do you know what she said when she found out I was going on this trip? She said, 'Isn't it nice to have a husband who's willing to babysit for that long?' Babysit! It's called *parenting*, Barb!"

"What did Dan say?" Katie asks.

"He agreed with me! He said he didn't see a difference between me going on this trip and him going on his business trip last month."

"Aww. Dan's a good guy," I say.

Beth's face softens. "Yeah, he is. He's the best."

I wave my hand in the air. "See, now why can't I find a guy like that?"

"Not for lack of trying," Katie mutters into her Coke.

"What's that supposed to mean?"

She smirks. "You go on enough dates."

I frown. "Yeah, but none of them are right for me. I just haven't been able to connect with anyone since ..." I frown and leave the sentence unfinished. My friends know who I mean and would rather I not bring him up.

I catch a loaded glance between Katie and Beth, and then Katie changes the subject. "So, what's our itinerary for the week?"

Beth grabs onto the new topic. "Well, tomorrow we'll go hiking to see some waterfalls, and beautiful fall leaves, hopefully. Wednesday, we're booked to go on a trail ride. The farm where we're staying offers them. Then on Thursday, we'll check out downtown and the River Arts District—shopping, eating, you know. And finally, Friday, we've got tickets for the Biltmore."

I squeal. "Ooh, I'm so excited to see the Biltmore! I love that Hallmark Christmas movie, you know, with the Biltmore and the ... what's it called?"

"Time travel?" Beth supplies.

"Yeah, the time travel."

The lavish Biltmore Estate, originally built by millionaire George W. Vanderbilt in the late 1800s, is a tourist destination in Asheville with a museum filled with art pieces the Vanderbilt family collected over the years and beautiful gardens on the grounds. I love the history of it, and I'm hoping to be inspired by the beautiful art collection and gardens. I need more inspiration in my life.

"This trip is going to be the best," I say, forecasting. "Thanks y'all, for coming with me and making my birthday special."

"We're happy to," says Katie, squeezing my shoulder. "You need this trip. Beth and I have both noticed you seem kind of down lately. Hopefully some girl time will help."

***

We're back at the vacation rental cottage by ten, and though it's early, I'm wiped out. Plus, I forgot one of the reasons I don't drink often is because it tends to make me morose. I'm not in the best head space for a fun vacation as I lie in bed thinking back over the evening.

Though Katie and Beth may have distracted me from my thoughts of the past earlier in the night, now the memories are so thick they cloud my vision, or maybe that's the champagne.

It's true I haven't felt like I connected with any of the men I've dated since college. Most of them were nice enough with decent jobs and good intentions. Still, the relationships always felt lacking, at least to me. No, the last time I truly connected with a man I was dating was in college. He was older than me, and when he graduated nine years ago, he broke my heart. To be fair, I don't think he did it intentionally, but it still hurt.

I try to sleep. It's hard when I'm wondering if I'll ever again meet someone I can be wholly myself with. My adult life hasn't turned out how I expected. I figured by now I'd be running a marketing team, focusing on video content that tells the story of a business, their mission, and their passion. Instead, I'm doing grunt work, writing copy under a taskmaster boss. I also thought I'd be married by now, like Beth, or at least close to it, like Katie. Thirty sounds like such a milestone birthday, but I'm stuck on a part of the road I should have passed ages ago.

***

The next few days are filled with activity and adventure. On Tuesday, we drive about an hour south to the DuPont State Forest and hike to three gorgeous waterfalls. It's too early in the season still for peak leaf peeping, but we see splashes of brilliant orange and deep red mixed in among the green on the trees as we walk. It's peaceful, the warble of birds in the trees overhead a fitting soundtrack to our trek. The loop is around three miles, and though I'm a city girl through and through and not a particularly apt hiker, the burn in my legs feels satisfying when we climb back into the car. My body is stronger, more at ease.

On Wednesday, we continue our outdoor adventures with a trail ride, booked through the farm where our cottage is located. The guide, an older woman named Cassie, takes us on foothill trails near the farm. She says the trail connects with the Mountains-to-Sea Trail, which is close by, and beyond that, the Blue Ridge Parkway. My horse is a brown mare named Ilsa, which I love because that's the name of one of the main characters in my favorite movie, *Casablanca*. Cassie knows where to find all the best fall leaves, so I have my phone out a lot, juggling it with the reins in my hand and trying to capture a fraction of the stunning color. I used to do summer day camps at the Atlanta Riding Club when I was a kid, so I'm no stranger to horses, but it's been a while. Ilsa seems sweet and calm, and I find I've missed horseback riding. I make a mental note to look for opportunities to ride when I get back home.

When we get back to the farm, Cassie warns us they're expecting a storm to come through Thursday night into Friday morning. "Some high winds and heavy rain," she says. "We're not close to a water source here so flooding probably won't be an issue. Ground saturation from the rain means we could get some downed trees. And electricity can be finicky out here."

Beth's eyebrows dip together in concern, and she shakes her head. "Thanks for letting us know. I'm sure we'll be fine. I'm glad we got our outdoor activities in while the weather was nice. Tomorrow we're just exploring downtown, and Friday we've got Biltmore tickets."

"That will be fun. Be sure to do the French Broad chocolate tour. It's my favorite." Cassie winks.

Katie and I look at Beth, who's been our primary trip planner. She smiles. "Yep, it's on our itinerary!"

"Good." Cassie grins. "Just be prepared for some rainy weather as you're exploring the city tomorrow."

***

Thursday starts out cloudy and dry. We park downtown and have an amazing breakfast before wandering in and out of shops. The chocolate tour is amazing, just like Cassie said. We watched each step of the chocolate-making process, tasting samples along the way.

The brown butter milk chocolate bar was my favorite, creamy with buttery caramel.

After lunch, the weather turns rainy, and Beth gets an email from the vacation rental host, Karen. It's mostly a warning similar to what Cassie told us yesterday: expect high winds and heavy rain tonight and tomorrow. We all have umbrellas, so we're not too worried. Our main plan for tomorrow is the Biltmore. The grounds are outside, of course, but I'm especially excited about the house tour, and the fancy birthday dinner we booked at The Dining Room, their upscale dining restaurant. My birthday isn't until Saturday, but I'm looking forward to celebrating Friday night at the Biltmore.

Closer to four, Beth's checking her phone again when she stops walking and mutters, "Uh oh."

"What's wrong?" Katie asks.

"I just got an email from the Biltmore. They're closing tomorrow because of the weather."

I frown. "Is that typical?"

"I'm not sure. It says they're reopening on Saturday, though."

Katie looks at me with raised eyebrows. "I know we're supposed to drive home Saturday. Maybe we can delay? Change our Biltmore tickets to Saturday and our reservations to lunchtime instead of dinner? We'll be home late Saturday night instead of afternoon, and then we don't have to miss out. I know you're looking forward to seeing the Biltmore."

"Sounds good to me." I turn to Beth. "Can we do that?"

"Works for me. I'll just call the phone number they give and get us rebooked."

Beth steps away to make the phone call.

"Should we be worried about this weather?" I ask Katie.

She shrugs. "I don't think so. If the Biltmore plans to reopen Saturday, I'm sure it will be fine. We can just hang around the cottage tomorrow and relax."

I look around at the wet, busy downtown streets. "You're right. The locals don't seem too concerned."

"Don't the mountains form a force field or something?"

I laugh. "A force field?"

"Yeah, like a climate safe haven. The mountains break up the storm, or whatever?"

"I don't know. Maybe?"

Beth rejoins us. She talked to someone at the Biltmore and successfully moved our tickets and dining reservations to Saturday lunch. "It works out better," Beth says. "Now we can visit the Biltmore on your actual birthday, Ramona."

True. This has been such a great trip already. I'm half in love with Asheville and the North Carolina mountains. I have no problem delaying going back to reality in Atlanta.

Chapter Two

Kevin

♥

I don't often come face to face with guests. My work is mostly behind the scenes when it comes to the vacation rental. I manage the bookings online and send messages, though the messages are in my mom's name, Karen. We get a lot of female guests, and they just feel more comfortable having a woman's name on the contact, and Mom does live on site, too. Sometimes I see the guests coming and going; there's not much in-person interaction.

So, it's unusual but not unheard of for me to see the vacation rental guests. Like now as I'm edging out of my truck and see an SUV pull into the parking spot for the cottage. They checked in on Monday, and here it is Thursday and it's the first time we've crossed paths. Again, not particularly surprising since I've been working in the back fields all week. A woman slides out of the vehicle—around my age, red hair. Wait. This woman looks familiar. She turns her face more in my direction and recognition sparks in my brain. Did I go to college with her? Kelly, Karrie, Connie, something like that. Wasn't she actually friends with— My train of thought is interrupted when another woman steps out—this one blonde—and I recognize her, too. I don't need to bumble for her name though since I know from the booking it's Beth. She was also friends with—

Again, I'm distracted when a third woman comes around the vehicle. I curse and quickly duck behind the cab of my truck to stay out of sight. I definitely know this woman. I would recognize her anywhere. Ramona Carpenter.

We didn't date long. We both insisted on keeping it casual, but for about six months during my senior year of college we were inseparable. We never said we were officially exclusive, though I don't know when either of us would have been seeing someone else since we spent all our free time together. We never labeled it; she was never actually my girlfriend. I knew clearly then, the same as I do now thinking back on it, that I was in love with her. I never told her.

She had a year of school left when I graduated and headed home to North Carolina to start training to take over the family farm so my dad could retire. Before I left, we agreed we weren't interested in trying anything long distance. Still, I contacted her a few times, and we texted back and forth as friends. Then one day she stopped responding, and I moved on. Or tried to. It's obvious to me I've measured any woman I've dated since against her. Ramona.

Now, some nine years later, she's here on my farm staying in the cottage I renovated myself. I take off my Atlanta Braves ball cap and flip it around so it sits backward on my head. I watch the three women unlock the cottage door and disappear inside, chatting and laughing. *Of all the gin joints in all the towns in all the world, she walks into mine.* Then immediately, I heave out a loud sigh. The only reason I know that quote is because Ramona made me watch *Casablanca*, and about a million other classic movies, when we hung out in college. I'm no Rick Blaine, but yeah, I became a little cynical about love and relationships when Ramona stopped texting me back all those years ago.

I've dated here and there. Mostly I've been busy on my family's horse farm, trying to keep it in the black. I get the sense my dad was more than happy to pass the business stuff on to me when I got home from college with a newly embossed business degree. A farm that's a "one-trick pony," if you'll excuse the pun, is sure to fail in today's economic market. I've been focusing on diversifying our services, tacking on (another horse pun) horse boarding and riding lessons, as well as more recently breaking into agritourism with trail rides and vacation rentals. We run horse day camps for kids in the summertime.

Speaking of the horses, I shake my head to clear my thoughts and get back to the task at hand. The forecast is calling for some bad weather overnight and tomorrow morning, and I need to make sure the barn is prepped and secure. I work for several hours to bring all the loose equipment into the barn, close off the empty stalls, and secure the fencing, windows, and doors. Once that's all done, I finish up the regular chores—or at least the ones my cousin Davie hasn't gotten to yet. I feed the horses, fill the troughs, and hang the hay nets in the stalls before closing the barn for the night. Though it's been drizzling all day, the rain is starting to pick up now, and I wipe my sleeve across my eyes every few minutes to clear the water away.

It's physical work, yet mindless, so it doesn't take much for my thoughts to drift back to Ramona and those short, intense months we spent together. I wonder what she's up to these days, if she's single. If we could reconnect after all this time. I know I've never gotten over her. It doesn't help that when I walk into the kitchen of my parents' farmhouse for dinner, the women staying in the cottage are the main topic of conversation.

"I took them on a trail ride yesterday and the weather was just perfect for it," my Aunt Cassie gushes. "The fall leaves aren't quite spectacular yet. Still, we saw plenty of colors to keep those city girls impressed."

I help my mom finish bringing the food to the table and settle into my chair—to the left of my dad, who sits at the head, and across from my mother—at the farmhouse table where I ate all my meals growing up. Cassie, who's my dad's sister, and her son, Davie—my idiot cousin who works with me at the farm and has a maturity level much younger than his twenty-six years—join us. Though I renovated and moved into a cabin on the property a year ago, it's convenient to eat dinner with my family here in the big house most nights.

"Where are they from?" I ask, feigning a casualness I don't feel, desperate for any information I can glean about where Ramona might be now and what she might be doing.

"They said Atlanta."

It makes sense Ramona would have stayed in Atlanta after college. She always loved the energy of the city, primed like she was for constant activity.

"They having a girls' trip?" my mom asks.

"Yep. One of them is celebrating a birthday, one of them is taking a break from planning her wedding, and one of them is taking a break from her husband and kids."

When is Ramona's birthday? Suddenly, remembering that piece of trivia from ten years ago seems like the most important thing I've ever had to do. Because if her birthday isn't now, she's either engaged or married. Just thinking of those possibilities makes my chest ache in a way I'm not ready to explain. She didn't celebrate a birthday while we were together, so that rules out December through May. Her birthday *could* be in September. Why didn't I think to check for a ring when I saw her outside earlier? That's right, I was too busy hiding behind my truck.

"They picked a beautiful week for it," my dad says. "It's finally starting to feel like fall out there."

"Which one's single?" Davie asks. Even while I roll my eyes at his question, I lean in to better hear the answer.

"Oh, gosh," Aunt Cassie sighs. "I can't remember. Wait, the blonde was the one with kids. She showed me a picture, and they're tow-headed just like her."

Okay, that would be Beth. Fifty-fifty chance Ramona's single now.

"And then the redhead is the one getting married, I think—"

"You *think*?" I practically shout. My parents, aunt, and cousin all turn to stare at me. I shrug. "I mean, oh, you think so?" I'm nonchalant, totally not invested in her response.

Aunt Cassie blinks at me, then continues her thought. "Anyways, yes, it was the redhead that had a gorgeous diamond engagement ring. Planning her wedding for New Year's Eve, she said."

I laugh out loud. The redhead would be Kelly or Connie or Carrie or whatever her name is, which means Ramona is here celebrating her birthday *and,* more than likely, she's single.

"That's so great!" I slap my hands against my thighs. Everyone's staring at me again. I ignore them and finish the meatloaf on my plate.

The dinner conversation moves on to the storm expected to come through overnight and into the morning. It'll be the remnants of a major hurricane either hitting Florida now or hitting Florida soon. Either way, by the time it gets to us it won't be more than a thunderstorm with some intense wind and rain. The mountains will break it up like they always do. We'll probably lose power, though, at least for a few hours, so it's a good thing the weather has cooled. We won't sweat to death.

I'm bone tired in body and heart after I run through the rain to my cabin after dinner. At the same time, I feel jittery. With the rain outside, I have no way of burning off my nervous energy, so I just take a shower and try to settle in for the night.

I fall asleep, tossing and turning, to *Casablanca* streaming on the TV. When the power goes out, sometime around two in the morning, it wakes me up. I roll out of bed and pull the blinds apart to look out the window. All I see is darkness and rain. The wind is loud, though. Really loud. Between the rain and the wind, we'll have some branches down in the morning. I rearrange my mental to-do list for tomorrow as I climb back into bed.

The next time I wake up, it's morning. The electricity is still off. Depending on how widespread the outages are it could be off all day. Power lines can be tricky in the mountains.

I get out of bed to peer through the blinds on my bedroom window. The sky is gray and cloudy, the rain has slowed to a drizzle. My bedroom is at the back of the cabin, so I can't see much of the farm from this vantage point. I can see a tree-covered hillside, where some smaller trees are down. Overall, it's not as bad as I expected. I pull on shorts and a shirt before making my way toward the front of the house, where I can see the farm in panorama from my front window.

The barn, out the window to the right, looks fine. I'll check on the horses and get them fed and watered later this morning. Straight out the window, across the fields, my parents' house sits steady as ever, Aunt Cassie's house right next door. We had a few of the older pine trees on the property removed last year, and it obviously helped because the number of branches on the ground is minimal. Out the window to the left, though ...

"What the—" I mutter to myself. I swipe the back of my hand across my eyes, dislodging the last of the sleep grit.

A giant oak tree has fallen. Fortunately, it didn't land on anything, but it *is* blocking the gravel road that is our neighbors' only way out. I put my shoes on to go investigate up close. Once the rain lets up, I'm sure this will be my first chore of the day. The horses will have to wait a little longer.

When I get to the tree, my dad's already there assessing. Standing right next to it, the tree is bigger than I thought. The trunk is easily four feet thick, and lying on its side, it's got to be half a football field long.

My dad grunts at me in greeting. "We'll have to get the road clear."

I nod back at him. My dad had a heart attack about six months ago and is still supposed to be taking it easy, so I hope what he means by "we" is "me," with him supervising from a lawn chair. He's been working on the farm his whole life, same as me, and has a hard time letting me take the lead on the physical labor.

"I'll get the chainsaws from the shed," I tell him.

He looks past me and raises his hand in greeting. I turn to see Jackson and Hud, two of the neighbors that live down the gravel road, approaching. They're middle-aged brothers, each with their own house and family on a large family acreage down the hill. They're holding chainsaws and looking ready to work.

"Morning, Kent, Kevin." Hud lifts his chin.

"Morning, Hud." Dad looks at me. "Kevin, run and get the chainsaws, and I'll pry your cousin out of bed to help."

When I get back with the chainsaws and an extra can of gas for when they run low, it's like walking into a party. Davie's here now, along with a handful of teenagers belonging to Jackson and Hud. Mr. Garner, another neighbor, brought his hacksaw and has started cutting some of the smaller branches off the main trunk. Mom, Aunt Cassie, and a few other neighbors have set up a folding table and stocked it with granola bars, fruit, and bottles of water.

I grin. This right here is one of the big reasons I could never leave the farm, or these mountains: the community. I hand a chainsaw to Davie, against my better judgment, and we get to work. It's not until a flash of movement in the window of the cottage catches my attention that I remember Ramona is here.

Chapter Three

Ramona

Between the busy week we've had and the gloomy weather outside, we all slept in this morning. Besides, without electricity—which went out sometime overnight—there wasn't much incentive to get out of bed. Now I'm up and showered, waiting for my friends to get dressed while I rummage through the kitchenette for something to eat for breakfast. Katie tried calling a local diner to see if they were open for brunch today. It rang and rang with no answer. So, our options are dry blueberry bagels—we already used up all the cream cheese—or a bag of tortilla chips. We can't have coffee, since the capsule coffee machine in the cottage needs power to work. I pour bottled water into a mug hoping for the placebo effect.

The drone of chainsaws outside pulls me toward the window. I look out to see a giant tree lying on its side blocking the gravel road past the farm. Several men and women are working on it with chainsaws, cutting it into manageable pieces to move to the side.

One man with his back to me catches my eye. A gray t-shirt sticks to his shoulders. As he moves, I can see every outline of his toned muscles stretching and flexing—and there's a lot to see. I watch for a few minutes. Something about the man looks familiar to me. He reminds me of someone; I can't figure out who.

His muscled back and arms make it clear he's no stranger to manual labor. A black ball cap covers his dark brown hair, the bottom edges shaggy against his neck. Below the gray t-shirt, dark wash jeans cover his backside and legs, tucked at his ankles into brown work boots. It's hard to tell without seeing his face, but he looks young, maybe around my age. Switching the chainsaw to one hand, he reaches his free hand up and slides his cap around. The front of the hat is a dirty white, with a lowercase red "a" outlined in black and white. The brim, black like the back of the hat, is bent and creased. I gasp.

About ten years ago, I bought a hat exactly like this one. Well, newer, of course. It was a graduation gift for the guy I was seeing at the time, Kevin. He was a huge Atlanta Braves fan and always wore a beat-up old Braves cap, so I thought he would appreciate a new one. I obsessed over that purchase, looking at dozens of options at the hat store in the mall until I found this one. The design was a special edition. Somewhere in the back of my mind I thought if I gave Kevin the perfect gift for graduation, it would communicate how important he was to me, though I never had the courage to say it in words.

For the few months we were together during my junior year of college, Kevin was everything to me. He was my first boyfriend, though he never called himself that. Anyway, he obviously meant more to me than I did to him because he graduated and left, texting me a couple of times, and then forgot all about me, I assume. Granted I was the one who insisted I didn't want a long-distance relationship. He returned to his family's business in ... North Carolina. I freeze.

Then, the man outside the window turns, and I can see the profile of his face. I nearly drop the mug I'm holding into the sink. Because it's him. Seriously, what are the odds? My breath catches, and I find myself sucking in air as if my lungs have forgotten how to work.

I resist the impulse to duck below the window and hide. First, he's not paying any attention to the cottage, and second, why would I need to hide? He's an old boyfriend from almost a decade ago. No big deal. As I think the words, my heart, thumping double time, belies them.

Kevin *was* a big deal in my life. We saw each other every day for a good six months, talked about everything, and shared so many amazing kisses. We met by chance at a coffee shop on campus when Katie recognized one of her classmates who was friends with Kevin and went over to talk to him. Beth and I followed, and we sat and chatted with the guys for an hour. I ended up next to Kevin, smiling shyly at him as we compared programs—he was a business major, and I was marketing. When I had to leave for class, he insisted on walking with me. It was unbelievable that the handsomest guy I'd ever seen wanted to walk *me* to class. We awkwardly said goodbye outside the building, and I sat through the lecture, zoned out, expecting I'd never see him again. When class ended, Kevin was outside waiting for me. He said, with a grin, that he had forgotten to get my number.

Katie comes up behind me and, resting her chin on my shoulder, she teases, "Enjoying the show?"

I know I should have some sort of saucy comeback, but I'm honestly still too astonished. Katie straightens and studies my face. I duck my head as I set the mug on the counter.

"Hey, are you okay?" She glances out the window, then back at me. Turning her eyes back to the scene outside, she watches for a few minutes. "Ra," she starts, her eyes wide, "is that—"

"Shhh!" I admonish her, as if the people outside can hear us.

She lowers her voice to a furious whisper. "Is that *Kevin King*? The Kevin you dated in college? The Kevin who totally ghosted you? The Kevin who broke your heart?" With each word, her voice gets louder until Beth comes out of the bedroom, where she's been talking on the phone with her family, to investigate.

"What's going on?"

"*Kevin's* outside," Katie shouts.

"Kevin?" Beth's eyebrows rise as her eyes narrow. "The Kevin Ramona was completely in love with in college who ruined her for all other men and then disappeared?"

Wow, seems extreme. I need this to not be the big thing my friends are making it into right now. If I can calm my whirling thoughts and sweaty palms, I can convince my heart Kevin has no place in it anymore.

"The very one," Katie confirms.

I raise my hands in a placating gesture. "You guys are exaggerating. I was *not* in love with Kevin. He *didn't* break my heart. And it's no big deal he's here, right outside, on my thirtieth birthday vacation."

My best friends stare at me.

"Really," I reassure them.

They watch me, and I arrange my expression into an unaffected and carefree smile. Then, almost simultaneously, Beth and Katie turn to watch Kevin outside the window.

All three of us stare at Kevin wielding a chainsaw to cut through the thick branches of the tree. Beth lets out a low whistle.

"The years have been good to him," she observes.

"Beth!" I gasp, reluctantly agreeing with her assessment as Katie laughs. "Oh my gosh, you're a married woman—and a mother!"

Beth shrugs. "Doesn't mean I don't have eyes … or a pulse."

I roll my eyes. Yes, Kevin is absolutely ripped, but should we be objectifying the guy?

"We should go out there, don't you think?" asks Katie. "Offer to help?"

"How could *we* help?" I ask.

Katie tilts her head and scrunches up her nose. "Moral support?"

I wring my hands. "What would I even say to him? After all this time?"

Beth sets her hands on my shoulders and guides me toward the door. "You can start with, 'Hey there. Remember me?'"

Before I have time to dwell on the fact that I'm wearing yoga pants with a pull-over hoodie (with the name of our shared *alma mater* on it, I realize with embarrassment), no makeup, and still-wet hair, I'm stepping onto the cottage's front porch, buoyed on either side by my best friends. We walk around the corner of the house until we're within ten feet of the tree and the crew working on dispatching it.

"Kevin, is that you?" Katie calls loudly. I elbow her in the ribs, hard.

He looks up, and as his eyes land on my face, he nearly drops the running chainsaw.

"Watch it, Kev!" Another man swears at him. "You tryin' to kill somebody?"

"Hey there. Remember me?" I ask with what I hope is a cool confidence to hide the thumping of my heart.

Despite his reaction, Kevin doesn't seem as surprised to see me as I was to see him. No, it's more a glint of panic, not shock, that appears in his eyes. Did he know I was here? Kevin turns off his chainsaw, waits until it stops, and hands it to another man standing behind him. Still watching me, he swipes the back of his hand across his brow and then his palms against the front of his jeans. He walks toward me as I see my friends quietly move away in my periphery.

"Hey," he says dumbly.

"Hi," I respond as he steps closer to me.

"It's, uh ... it's good to see you, Ramona."

I crook an eyebrow. "Is it?" I ask. I take in his tense posture and the barely concealed fight-or-flight instinct glimmering in his eyes.

"Well, I just ..." he trails off. "Uh, it's been a long time."

"Nine years," I say softly.

"Yeah."

"So, you live around here?" I ask.

"Yeah. Over there actually." He sheepishly points to the pretty blue cabin I admired earlier. He shrugs. "This is my family's farm."

"Oh," I say, because I can't think of a better response. I'm turning this new information over in my mind.

"I was going to check on y'all right after we got this tree taken care of," he continues.

My brain might be short circuiting. "You were going to check on us," I repeat.

He lifts his hat and runs a hand through his hair, watching my face with a grimace. "I manage the vacation rentals," he explains.

I shake my head. "No, we've been messaging with a woman named Karen."

He grimaces again. "My mom," he says. "We put her name and picture on the bookings, but it's me who does the messaging. And the bookings and the cleaning." He chuckles.

"Oh," I say again. "You don't seem surprised to see me."

"I saw you yesterday when you got home," he admits. "I was surprised then."

"You ... didn't want to say hi?" My wavering voice exposes my disappointment. My stupid heart must still be holding out hope that I've been on his mind as much as he's been on mine these last nine years. My body gears up for a battle between emotion and logic. For me, logic almost always wins ... except when it comes to Kevin.

A cloud passes over his face, and he looks at his shoes. "I didn't know how."

I take the opportunity to consider his face. Beth's right. The years since college have been good to him. He looks the same—same handsome face and sharp jawline, same light blue eyes and thick eyebrows—just older. He has stubble across his face where he always used to be clean-shaven. He has a weight in his eyes where he always used to exude joy and mischief. His body was always fit, but he's heavier now, sturdier. His arm and shoulder muscles reflect the strength of someone accustomed to carrying ... I don't know, bales of hay and bags of feed, or something.

Kevin glances behind him at the progress on the tree. "Hey, they're about done here. Come with me to the barn while I take care of the horses. I'd like to catch up." He catches and holds my eye. "Talk?"

My brain, still catching up, wants to put the brakes on this run-away train. Kevin's always had a power over me. Like when we were together, the rest of the world didn't exist. Like we didn't need anything else.

"Sure," I find myself saying. *Sure? Why would I agree just like that? One point for emotion.*

He grins, and any thoughts of brakes or caution fly straight out of my mind. He's *here*, and he wants to talk to *me*.

"This way." He tilts his head toward the barn and starts walking in that direction. Before following, I turn to find Beth and Katie. They're watching me, so I give them a wave. Beth raises her eyebrows, and I smile. She says something to Katie, whose lips are pinched.

Kevin stops walking and looks back at me. "You comin'?"

Chapter Four

Ramona

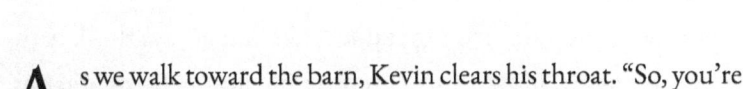

A s we walk toward the barn, Kevin clears his throat. "So, you're still in Atlanta."

It's a statement, not a question, and I wonder how he knows.

"Yeah."

"What do you do there?"

I pause before answering, looking up at the mountain and determining how much to share. "I work at a luxury marketing firm, Prestige Strategies."

"That's great. Marketing is what you were studying for." He smiles at me.

"Mhmm."

"You don't like it?"

I bobble my head. "Sure. It's fine." I hate it, but Kevin doesn't need to know that.

"Do you do anything with video marketing? You minored in film, didn't you?"

I pop my head up to look at him. "You remember?"

He holds my gaze and then looks away. Softly, he says, "I remember a lot."

Well, that's confusing. Isn't he the one who ghosted me? All these years, I know I've thought about him. Often. I never figured he's been using any brain power on me. Maybe he has.

He grins. "And anyway, you made me watch enough old movies."

"*Made* you?" I scoff.

"Yeah, well, it wasn't *too* much of a hardship." He winks and my irresponsible heart skips a beat.

We get to the barn. It's big and red, like you always think barns will be. Honestly, I haven't spent much time around barns or farms. I grew up in the suburbs of Atlanta, then moved farther into the city the older I got. I like that there's always something to do—a new restaurant to try or a concert to attend. I'm not sure I've ever been in a real barn. The front of the barn has giant, picturesque sliding doors, but Kevin leads me around to the side and opens a normal-sized door for us to enter.

Not only does Kevin's barn look how I expect it to look, it also smells how I expect it to smell. I look around. There are stalls along both sides. Six are currently occupied. I recognize the horses Katie, Beth, and I rode during our trail ride the other day. My horse, Ilsa, was brown. Katie rode Princess, I think, and Beth had Laszlo.

"I met these three on my trail ride the other day," I tell Kevin. "What are the others named?"

Kevin points to a large horse that looks almost red. "That's Clifford." He gestures to another horse that's brown with white spots, almost like a cow. "This one is Gertrude. They're not ours. We board them." He walks to the far corner, where a beautiful white horse greets him with a whinny. "And this is my best guy, Blaine."

Wait a minute. I run through the horses' names again in my mind. I frown, my chest tightening.

"Ilsa and Blaine?"

Kevin looks away, then flips his hat around on his head to face forward. "Uh, yeah."

"Like from *Casablanca*?"

"Yeah. Laszlo, too. And Princess for *Roman Holiday*."

My eyebrows squish together. "Your horses are named after characters from classic movies?"

"Yeah. Want to help me feed them?"

I want to push and ask more. I have so many questions. Does *he* name the horses? Why classic movies? He'd never seen any of the old classics until we watched them together in college. The first time we kissed, *Casablanca* was playing in the background, which only clinched it as my favorite movie. It's too much of a trip down memory lane, so I let it drop.

"Definitely."

I help Kevin fill buckets with pellets for each horse, and we hang them inside the stalls. The horses start eating right away. Kevin explains that he's usually in here first thing, like six in the morning, to feed them, but the tree took precedence today.

A metal water trough runs the length of the barn. It has a spigot on each end to replenish the water, which Kevin says needs to happen often. He turns the handle; the faucet sputters as if searching for the water that's supposed to gush out, but nothing comes. He frowns and walks to the other end to try the second spigot. Again, the pipes gurgle, and no water flows.

"That's weird." Kevin flips his hat around on his head and squats to inspect the pipes connected to the faucet.

While he works, I pull out my phone to give Beth and Katie an update. I type out a text, but my phone tells me the message can't be delivered. I switch over to a social media app. It won't load either. Finally, I look at the top, right corner of my screen, and there's a circle with a line through it where it normally shows the signal strength. I furrow my brows. "Huh."

Kevin tilts his head up to see me. "What?"

"Is your phone working?" I ask.

He stands and pulls his phone from his pocket while he walks closer to me. He studies the screen, then frowns. "No."

"Do you usually have service in the barn?"

"Yeah, usually we have no problem anywhere on the farm." He gives me a wry look. "I know you're used to the city, but we're not that remote out here."

"No water and no phone service," I muse, ignoring his quip. "Is it because of the storm?"

"No," he protests, his eyes widening. "I mean, no. Right? We've never lost water before."

I shrug.

"Let's go find out." Kevin grabs my hand and leads me out of the barn toward the large, gray-paneled house on the other side of the property. My palm prickles with the contact of his skin against mine.

It would be so easy to lean into the feeling. Instead, my logical brain clicks into place, and I gently pull my hand loose.

He stops walking. "Sorry."

"It's fine. Let's go."

We continue, and soon I'm standing in the kitchen of what I presume is Kevin's childhood home. Two women, and a man who looks like an older, grayer version of Kevin, sit at the kitchen table with grave faces. I recognize one of the women as Cassie, who led our trail ride.

"There's no water in the barn," Kevin blurts.

They shift in their seats to look at him, their expressions ranging from curious to dazed as they notice me standing with him.

"No water anywhere," Cassie responds. "Not for the last hour." Kevin tilts his head at her.

"Have you listened to the radio at all, son?" the man asks.

"No. I've been ...," Kevin stops and looks at me, "... in the barn feeding the horses."

Nobody says anything for a few moments. "Dad?" Kevin prods.

"Well, I took the truck out to drive around. I figured if we have a tree down, others might, too." Kevin's father shakes his head. "It's bad. Whole trees and power lines are down all over. I couldn't get through on some roads, though folks were out there with their chainsaws, same as us."

"From the storm last night?" Kevin asks.

He grunts. "It gets worse. I had the radio on, and well, most of the stations are playing songs and such as normal. I searched around until I found one talking about Asheville. It was a briefing from the authorities. No one has power. No one has water. There's some sort of issue with one of the water treatment plants. I didn't hear the whole thing. They were talking about how teams have been out all morning doing swiftwater rescues."

I don't understand the term or the implication, but I see on Kevin's face the moment realization dawns for him. "Flash floods," he says.

His dad nods. "I was able to get out onto the main road. The part of 74 next to the Swannanoa River is blocked though. It's underwater."

Kevin sinks slowly into an empty chair. I resist the impulse to put my hand on his shoulder. I'm not following the conversation fully, but I understand something has happened, something bad.

"Do we know how bad it is?" he asks. "How widespread?"

His father shakes his head. "I tried to search up more information; nothing's working. All they said on the radio was 'consider all roads closed.'"

Kevin lets out his breath. "I saw the flash flood alerts when they popped up on my phone this morning. I didn't think ... I never thought ..."

I clear my throat. "I'm so sorry to interrupt. What's happening, exactly?"

Kevin jumps up. "Oh! Sorry. Everyone, this is Ramona. She's one of the guests staying in the cottage. We, uh, know each other from college ... uh, coincidentally." His eyes shift to me awkwardly before he turns back toward his family. "Ramona, this is my mom and dad, Kent and Karen, and my Aunt Cassie."

The woman Kevin introduced as his mother is tall and thin with short gray hair and the same light blue eyes as her son. She gazes at me with raw curiosity before turning back to her son. "Ramona?" she asks. "Is this the same Ramona—"

Kevin cuts her off. "Yep, probably the same person you're thinking of." He chuckles mirthlessly. "What a great memory you have, Mom ... unfortunately." The last part he mumbles under his breath.

I pinch my lips together to hold back a smile. The fact that Kevin's mother recognizes my name is interesting information, though I wonder if what she's heard is positive.

"To answer your question, dear," Cassie says. "The wind and rain seem to have caused mass havoc on our mountain town. We don't know the extent yet, but if there's no electricity, water, or cell service, it can't be good. That's never happened before."

I take in her words, still not quite sure what's happening. "Okay. Well, I'm glad I took a shower already this morning, at least."

Kevin groans. "I didn't."

Kevin's mom rises from her seat at the table and shuffles over to the kitchen counter, where she rifles through one of the boxes stacked there. She hands Kevin something.

"Wet wipes," she explains. "You better get scrubbing."

***

I leave Kevin to his washing and head back to the cottage to find my friends. I update them on what's going on, or at least what I know.

"I don't think the Biltmore is going to reopen tomorrow," I finish.

Katie's forehead creases. "That sounds bad, Ra. Maybe we should drive home."

"That's a good idea," Beth says. "With phone service out, I can't get a hold of Dan anymore. I don't want him to worry."

Katie agrees. "Plus, with no electricity, no water, and nothing to do, we can't finish out our vacation anyway."

They both turn to look at me. I shrug. "I'm not sure it's possible to leave. Kevin's dad said something about all roads being closed."

They exchange a look. "Kevin's dad said that, huh?"

"Yes."

"All roads closed sounds kind of unlikely. There are major highways in and out of here. They can't possibly all be closed." Katie raises her eyebrows.

I shrug. "That's what he said."

"Or do you not want to leave?" Katie challenges.

Selfishly, I *don't* want to leave. Being back in Kevin's presence is like a sugar rush, and I'm not looking forward to the inevitable crash.

Beth holds up her hand. "Let's turn on the radio. We can listen for information about driving out."

The only radio we have is in Beth's SUV, so we pile in to listen. The floorboards are still littered with the remnants of our idyllic first few days in Asheville: leaves that had stuck to our shoes on the hike now cling to the carpet, shopping bags from our day in town are bunched behind the driver's seat.

Katie scans through the stations until she comes across one that sounds like it's broadcasting a media briefing from officials. We're coming in part way through, but we get the gist. There has been lots of flooding, even mudslides, and as Kevin's dad said, the officials urge listeners to "consider all roads closed." Including the major highways, apparently. We don't know what obstacles we might encounter getting to the highway, never mind once we're on it. Plus—

"Beth, how much gas do we have?" I twist and lean in my seat to see the dashboard.

Beth looks at the gauge. "Um, only about one hundred miles worth."

How far can we get on one hundred miles of gas? Obviously, one hundred miles, give or take, but where would that take us?

"I'm going to take a wild guess no gas stations here are open, and so we'd need those one hundred miles of gas to last us until we found one that is," Beth says.

We're all silent.

Finally, I lead off with, "What I'm about to say has *nothing* to do with Kevin. Pinky swear. *But* we know we're safe right here, if not exactly comfortable, so it's probably best to stay until we know better what we're dealing with. I'd hate to get stranded somewhere out of gas or use up the gas we have trying to find a way out."

By the looks on my friends' faces, I know they agree with me. It's not ideal, but it's the best plan we have so far.

Katie drums her fingers against the dashboard. "Except ... what about food? And water? We're running low on both."

A quick rap against my window makes us all jump. I look up to see Kevin, a frown on his face. He's changed into fresh jeans and a new t-shirt, this one the same cornflower blue as his eyes. Katie already turned off the car, so I open the door to talk to him.

"Yes?"

"You ladies aren't driving anywhere, are you?"

I shake my head. "Listening to the radio, trying to make a plan."

His face softens, and he lets out a breath. "Listen, it doesn't sound like it's safe to be out and about. You're welcome to stay here as long as you need to. We have plenty of food and bottled water."

"Are you sure?" Beth asks.

"Positive. Please stay."

"It doesn't seem like we have much choice," Katie grumbles.

Kevin grins at that. "This place isn't so bad." His eyes catch and hold on mine. "We'll take care of you."

Chapter Five

We walk with Kevin to his parents' house, where he's promised us lunch. After half a dry bagel and a handful of tortilla chips for breakfast, I'm starving. The closer we get to the house, the more I notice a low droning noise.

Kevin points to the field behind the house. "Generator," he explains. "I got it hooked up to power the kitchen, mostly. You can charge your phones if you need to."

Beth looks at him eagerly. "I'd love to charge my phone. I know there's no reception right now, but I want to be ready when there is."

"Beth has two little ones at home," I explain. "She's anxious about not being able to contact them."

Kevin dips his head. "I can understand that."

"What about you?" I prompt. "Are your friends or ... girlfriend ... or anyone going to be worried?"

Katie rolls her eyes, and Kevin smirks. "Nope. This farm is pretty much my whole world. My family and my horses are right here, and I've already checked in with all of them."

I hide a smile as we walk up the porch steps and through the side door to the kitchen. Not that it matters whether he has a girlfriend, I remind myself. I'm only here a few more days, I hope, and then it's back to my life two hundred miles away.

We make sandwiches with deli meat and cheese from the refrigerator. Beth plugs in her phone. Then the four of us—I'm not sure where the rest of Kevin's family is—sit around the kitchen table and talk. Beth and Katie share what they've been up to since college, and Kevin tells us more about the farm. He keeps stealing glances at me, like he can't believe I'm here. I get it. *I* can't believe I'm here. On Kevin's farm of all places.

The conversation lulls, and Katie stands. "Well, we'd better get back to our cottage. Thanks for lunch."

Beth and I move to follow her, while Kevin jumps out of his seat.

"Wait," he says, eyes on me. "Do you want to help me in the barn? With the horses?"

Katie clears her throat, and Kevin glances at her and Beth. "All of you are welcome to help."

I can't keep the smile off my face as I answer him. "I'd love to."

"Ramona," Katie says, pulling on my arm. "Can I talk to you privately for a moment, please?"

Katie pulls me into the entryway. Beth unplugs her phone and joins us, holding it up while she looks for any kind of signal.

"I'm just going to help him with the horses," I tell them.

Katie groans. "Here we go again."

"What?"

"In college you totally disappeared when you were dating Kevin. You two were obsessed with each other. We didn't see you for practically a whole semester."

"It's not like we hung out the same amount after Beth got married, or when you started dating Jonah. Why don't I get to have that?"

"Ramona, what's your endgame here?" Beth asks quietly.

"No endgame. We're just two old friends catching up, that's all."

"Yeah," Katie scoffs. "You two were never just friends."

"Why are you being like this?"

Katie's eyes flash. "We're trapped here, in the middle of an emergency in these stupid mountains, and you go off to flirt with your college boyfriend?"

I lower my voice. "There's nothing we can do right now. We can't leave. We might as well find some way to pass the time until that changes."

"Fine." Katie stomps out of the house and down the porch steps toward the cottage.

Beth puts her hand on my arm. "I'll talk to her. You're right. We might as well make the most of things. Be careful, okay?"

I shrug. "It's not storming anymore."

Beth gives me a pointed look. "That's not what I mean."

I know I should be careful. There is a storm still brewing here, but it's not outside. I'm putting myself in danger of being as into Kevin as I ever was, and it can only end badly.

When I step back into the kitchen, Kevin stands leaning against the counter.

"How much did you hear?" I ask.

"Um..."

"So, all of it?"

"Katie was *not* trying to be quiet."

I grimace. "Sorry. I think we're all feeling stressed."

Kevin shakes his head. "It's fine. I'm happy to help you 'pass the time.'" He pinches his lips together.

Inwardly, I cringe. That's what I said, but in all honesty, I was trying to downplay things in front of Katie and Beth. Spending time with Kevin means way more to me than simply passing time until we can leave Asheville. I can't tell him that either.

"So, uh, what do we need to do for the horses?"

He sighs. "They need water. Come on."

As I follow behind him, I'm curious how we're going to give the horses water without the spigots working. Dump a thousand bottles of water into the trough?

Kevin leads me back to a small garage near the barn. He pulls the door open and reveals a vehicle that looks like a golf cart designed for off-roading. It's about the size of a golf cart, but it has big tires with deep treads and a small bed in the back.

"Hop in."

I climb into the passenger seat, and Kevin drives us around the back of the barn where a row of large rain barrels is set up to catch the outflow of water from the rain gutters. Kevin pulls a stack of buckets out of the bed of the golf cart and explains how we need to fill the buckets from the rain barrels and transport them back to the barn on the UTV—which apparently is what the fancy golf cart is called—to then pour into the trough.

"There's a way to attach a hose to the rain barrel," Kevin explains. "We're not set up for it right now. We'll do it the hard way today, and then I'll work on the hose for next time."

"Is it safe for the horses to drink this water?"

Kevin squints his eyes and flips the hat around on his head. "It's not ideal. Out here, the rainwater is clean enough. We washed out the rain barrels recently. And it's better than having no water at all for them." He shrugs.

My questions answered, we get to work. It's not hard—we're not carrying the buckets far—but it is tiring. I'm squatting and lifting and then doing it all over again. It's better than a Pilates class.

Kevin grins at me. "Doin' okay?"

"Yeah, fine."

"I'm sure you're not used to this kind of work, are you, city girl?" Kevin normally has a slight Appalachian accent; he's exaggerating it now while he teases me.

I roll my eyes, not answering. Though it's true at home my physical activity comes mostly from machines at the gym, I'm not exactly out of shape. To prove my mettle, I take a bucket in each hand and lift them both into the bed of the UTV at the same time. I toss an exultant look over my shoulder at Kevin.

He chuckles and holds up his hands. "I stand corrected."

I turn back toward the rain barrels and ruin the effect of my double-bucket moment by tripping over a tree root. I brace myself to hit the ground. In a split-second, Kevin's strong arms are around my waist, keeping me upright.

"Careful." His voice sounds gruff, and I can feel his breath on my ear. My heart pounds as I turn my head.

"Thank you," I murmur. I'm looking straight into his eyes. We're so close I can feel the vibrations in his throat as he swallows. Our mouths are only inches apart. It would be so easy to lean in and kiss him. Would it feel the same as in college? I remember the all-consuming heat of his lips. I could never get enough. I'm hungry—and terrified—to taste him again.

The fear that thought causes is enough to shake me out of my paralysis. I take a step back, placing my hands on Kevin's arms and nudging him away. He drops his hands from my waist and backs up. My cheeks are on fire, so I press my cool fingers against them.

"We should, uh, finish up here." Kevin's face is impassive, except for the intense heat in his eyes.

I retreat further away from him, my eyes watching the ground. "Yeah, we've got some thirsty horses waiting on us."

We finish filling and loading the buckets and drive them to the front of the barn, where Kevin gets out and opens the large sliding doors to pull the UTV inside. We reverse our process and empty each bucket into the trough.

The horses are grateful for the water, chuffing their appreciation and taking long drinks.

I run my hand across Ilsa's side, up to her neck where I scratch her gently. "Do you remember me?" I ask her softly. "From our ride the other day?" She nickers, which I take to be a yes.

"She likes you," Kevin says. "See how relaxed she is? She trusts you."

For some reason, it feels like the victory I need. I'm underappreciated at work. My dating life is so pathetic that I'm pining over my ex-boyfriend from college. I'm turning thirty tomorrow with little to show for it, but gosh darn it, this horse trusts me.

Kevin starts stacking the buckets, so I grab a few and help.

"My family's having a bonfire tonight," he says. "We'll roast hotdogs for dinner. My mom said something about baked beans, too. Everyone's invited."

"Sounds fun."

He stops working and turns to me, tucking his hands into the back pockets of his jeans. "Come with me." His eyes don't leave mine.

"Come with you? I thought you said everyone is invited."

"They are. You are. I mean, I hope you'll come either way. But, you know, arrive with me, sit with me. Be with me at the bonfire. I'd love to talk to you more. Catch up. Just ... spend time with you, Ramona."

I think about how electric his hand felt in mine that morning, the warmth of his breath on my ear and the heat of his arms around my waist when he stopped me from falling earlier. I want this too much, which is exactly how I know it's a bad idea. I'm not sure I can trust Kevin not to hurt me again. I'm not sure I can trust myself not to let him.

I take a step back. "I'll come with Katie and Beth, and we can all sit together." I drop my eyes, knowing he's still watching me.

"Deal." His disappointment is palpable in the drop of his voice. He picks up the stack of buckets and quickly turns toward the barn entrance.

I follow him out. After dropping the buckets in the bed of the UTV, he motions toward his cute blue cabin. He steps away, creating space between us. "I better go get cleaned up. I'll see you at dinner. Thanks for your help today."

"Yeah," I say weakly. "You're welcome."

Without a glance back, Kevin heads for home. My thoughts are muddled. He's being attentive and flirty, giving no indication he remembers we lost touch so abruptly in college, offering no explanations. I shake my head back and forth, pinching my eyes shut.

I get back to our cottage to find Katie pacing on the front porch and Beth relaxing on a patio chair reading. Or trying to. They're both eager to fill me in on what I've missed.

"We had two water deliveries while you were gone," Katie tells me with no trace of her previous agitation. "The woman who took us for the trail ride the other day—"

"Cassie," I supply.

"Yes, Cassie. She brought us a case of bottled water to drink."

I'm confused as to why Katie included the "to drink" part, because what else would we do with it?

"And then," she continues, "a *delightful* man named Dave or something brought us two large orange buckets of nonpotable water." Her inflection on "delightful" tells me he wasn't at all.

"What are the buckets of water for?" I ask.

"Oh, I'm so glad you asked. They are for manually flushing the commode. As this *splendid* gentleman explained to us while simultaneously hitting on me and insulting me: 'If it's yellow, let it mellow; if it's brown—'"

I hold up my hands. "I get it."

Katie returns to her pacing. I look at Beth with a question in my eyes.

"Katie is feeling like a caged tiger," Beth explains. "Restless, anxious—"

"Trapped," Katie finishes. "Totally and completely trapped."

I motion to the view of the mountains in the distance. "But what a beautiful prison."

Katie scoffs while I sit next to Beth. I mean it, though. Before the storm, I loved everything we saw and experienced in this town. Even now, when I could be stressed out like Katie, the work I did with Kevin and the peaceful ambience of the mountains have me feeling calm. I haven't felt this way in Atlanta in a long time.

"Dinner tonight is hotdogs roasted over a campfire," I tell my friends.

Katie perks up. "With s'mores?"

I shrug. "I'm not sure. I guess that would depend on whether the Kings have marshmallows and graham crackers and chocolate bars handy. It's not like they can go to the store."

The latest radio update didn't provide any new information about the status of the world outside King Farms. It's more of the same: consider all roads closed. Stay home. Businesses remain closed.

***

Apparently, the Kings keep a well-stocked pantry because along with hot dogs and baked beans, there's cornbread, jars of pickles, potato salad, and yes, to Katie's delight, all the fixings for s'mores.

More people are here than I expected. In addition to the King family, several other families are present; neighbors I would guess. It's a real community gathering, and despite the uncertainty and the stress of the day, the atmosphere is cheerful. Laughter wafts into the sky along with plumes of smoke from the bonfire.

Kevin waves us over, and we sit on the log bench between him and a group of teenagers. As much as I try to be present with my friends, my attention is drawn back again and again to the man sitting on my right. He's changed clothes again—probably not the best idea considering who knows when he'll have water to wash a load of laundry—red joggers with a black Henley shirt and a gray zippered hoodie with the Atlanta Braves logo across the front. No ball cap. Instead, his brown hair curls around his ears, giving him a boyish appeal and rolling back the years to the Kevin I knew in college. We eat and talk as the sky gets darker around us. At one point, Beth taps me on the shoulder and lets me know they're heading back to the cottage. I tell them I won't be much longer.

Kevin and I talk about things of little importance, avoiding topics like feelings or heartbreak or why he stopped texting me all those years ago. Instead, we talk about hobbies, new ones we've picked up since college and lifelong ones we still enjoy. We talk about our families, like how Kevin's older sister is married and mother to his niece and nephew. We talk about names—how my mother, a children's librarian, named me after Ramona Quimby of the Beverly Cleary books, and how once his mother, Karen, married Kenton King, it became her goal to give them all matching names: Kenton, Karen, Kristen, and Kevin King.

I laugh. "You'll have to marry someone whose name starts with a K, or she'll be disappointed."

He groans. "You mean, keep the tradition going?"

I shrug. "Why not? Your children can be Kameron and Kayden. Ooh, or Kayson."

"Killian," Kevin adds. "Or Kieran and Karson."

"See? Lots of options."

"And what if I fall in love with a woman whose name starts with something else?" His eyes are guarded as he inches closer to me on the bench. I look around; everyone else has gone inside, and the fire has burned to embers. The night is quiet, and the sky stretches out above us, inky black broken up by sparkling stars.

I shiver and Kevin pulls me closer, wrapping his arm around my shoulders. I sink into his side, inhaling. The man smells better than anyone who's been working outside all day without a proper shower has a right to. It's a mixture of laundry detergent and campfire smoke and cool autumn air.

"That's not allowed," I hear myself say. "You'll have to save yourself only for women with K names."

He leans closer and whispers in my ear. "What's your middle name?"

I chuckle. "Kathryn. With a K." I tilt my head back to look in his eyes, the reflection of firelight and stars bright enough for me to see them soften and spark. My eyes dart to his lips as he angles closer.

I pull back and he stops, his arm still around me. My thoughts are spinning out of control. How did I get here? How have I gone from carefree traveler this morning to the cusp of kissing my college boyfriend tonight? I shouldn't kiss him. Of course I shouldn't. Before today, I hadn't seen him for nine years. We don't know anything about each other anymore.

He rests his forehead against mine. "Am I reading this wrong?" he asks, his voice raw.

All my senses and emotions are heightened. My heart beats double time; I can feel it through my whole being. I also feel each point where Kevin's body is in contact with mine, a searing heat that brands me as his, despite how ridiculous that sounds after being apart for so many years. But in this moment, I know my logical brain can't tell me anything that's going to stop me from kissing Kevin, whether it's a good idea or not. Nothing in the world could stop me.

I shake my head and whisper, "No."

He leans closer, slowly bringing his lips to mine. The contact is feather-light, testing, teasing. I incline my head, bringing our faces closer together. My lips press into his, and he pushes back, increasing the pressure. His arm around my shoulder drops to encircle my waist, pulling me closer. My hand darts up to the curls around his face before moving around to the back of his neck. I swear it's like muscle memory kicks in. Which means this kiss, like my feelings, gets way too intense way too quickly for a reintroduction after almost a decade. When we break apart, we're both breathing heavily. He rests his forehead back against mine.

"It's a little late to ask," Kevin whispers. "You don't have a boyfriend, do you?"

I laugh. "Not at all."

He grins. "Well, in that case..." His lips find mine again, and I'm utterly lost.

Chapter Six

Kevin

♥

I whistle as I tackle my chores the next morning, chores that are ten times more difficult now without electricity or running water. Nevertheless, I feed the horses and get a hose hooked up to the rain barrels, all the while whistling like a bird.

I'm up early—have to be on a farm. The morning is gorgeous, sunny and cool with a sparkling sheen of dew on the grass. I wouldn't have guessed the weather tried to kill us just twenty-four hours ago.

Of course, the more I think about that kiss with Ramona—and the several more that followed before I finally walked her to the cottage door—the brighter and more magical the new day appears.

I've been greedy with her time. It's never enough for me. She's giving it willingly, though.

It's like ... I don't know, like a piece of my soul has been missing for the last nine years and kissing her put it back into place. Well.

Maybe I'm getting carried away. I never thought I'd see her again, let alone kiss her and have a second chance with her.

And what a kiss...

I'm trying not to think too far ahead, but my plan right now is to spend as much time with Ramona as possible before she has to go back to Atlanta; before it's possible for her to go back to Atlanta.

Lingering in the back of my mind are the worries and apprehensions about what might be going on in the rest of Asheville and the mountains of western North Carolina. Despite the blatant reminders in the form of no utilities and the remnants of the giant tree we cut up yesterday still lying in the field, it feels far away, somehow. Like we're in this bubble of safety and ignorance. I'd like to keep it that way indefinitely, but I know we can't hide forever.

I'm distracted from this line of thought when the barn door opens and Ramona and her friends walk in.

Ramona approaches me first, Beth and Katie (I know it's Katie now, after hearing it several times yesterday) hanging back. My cheeks hurt for how wide I'm smiling. She looks up at me shyly, tossing a quick glance over her shoulder at her friends. Katie scowls.

"Mornin', beautiful lady."

Ramona blushes. "Hey."

"Oh, for the love of ... Ramona, can you just ask him?" Katie snaps.

Ramona frowns. "Yeah. Yep. Sorry." She clears her throat. "Kev, the girls were talking to that group of teenagers last night—"

"Jackson and Hud's kids from down the hill," I insert.

"Anyway. They were saying there's a shopping plaza down the road somewhere with a hardware store and a McDonald's, and the parking lot there is the best place for cell reception. Beth is eager to get in touch with her family and Katie ... well, Katie wants to try to find more information on leaving. Can you give us directions to the plaza?"

So much for my enclave of peace away from reality. "I'll do you one better. I'll take you there myself."

"Oh, you don't have to," Beth protests.

"Nah, it's fine. We've been kind of isolated out here. I should try to find out more of what's happening myself. When do you want to go?"

"As soon as possible," Katie says.

I look around the barn to make sure I've done the tasks I need to for now.

"Sure. Give me five minutes? I'll meet you by my truck. It's the black one out front."

Beth and Katie file out of the barn, Ramona hanging back. I grin at her expectantly.

"You doin' okay?" I ask.

"Yeah. I just ... I want to make sure we're on the same page."

"What page are you on?" My heart thumps, and I brace myself for her to backpedal.

"The page where I want to spend as much time with you as possible before we go back to Atlanta."

I exhale in relief. "Baby, we're one hundred percent on the same page."

I never called her by any pet names back in college. I never felt like I could since our relationship was nebulous and unofficial, so I held back. Where we are now is nebulous, too, but I have no interest in holding back this time. I won't make the same mistakes. Calling her "baby" feels right to me. Authentic.

She beams at me, and I hook my arm around her waist, pulling her against me. I kiss her deeply and quickly release her.

"Your friends will be waiting all day if you get me going with all that." I wink.

Ramona rolls her eyes. They're twinkling as she says, "You started it."

And I'd like to finish it, too. I don't say that part out loud.

"I'll be there in a minute. I need to grab my phone and keys from the cabin."

In record time, I'm at the truck where I see the ladies waiting for me. We pile in. Ramona sits up front with me, while Beth and Katie take the back seat.

As I start up the long gravel road that leads out of our alcove, I feel suddenly nervous. This is the first time I've left the farm since the storm. If my dad's reports are any indication, it could be rough out here. I'm worried about what we'll see and what it means for our area.

As soon as I pull onto the paved road that runs through the neighborhood adjoining us, we get an eyeful—trees lie across the pavement, branches tangled in power lines. Most have been cut apart, like we did yesterday with the big tree on our property, to clear a path for vehicles. Still, I drive slowly. The pace not only lets me survey the damage but also makes sure I'm traversing the obstacles safely. Downed trees have taken out fences, and even the roofs of houses in some cases. Power lines coil on the road and the shoulder like thick black snakes.

We turn onto a busier road and, of course, all the stop lights are out. Again, I drive cautiously. Seems like many of my fellow drivers either don't know or don't care to treat the intersections like four way stops. We pass a corner store—a local place where you can normally pick up fishing bait and ice along with your case of beer—with a line out the door and around the corner. No way they have power. They're open—I'm assuming cash only—to sell what supplies they have on hand.

As we keep driving, everything else is closed. I turn left into the shopping plaza the ladies mentioned, and sure enough, the parking lot is teeming with cars and people walking around with cell phones in hand. If we had kept going a few hundred yards down the road, we would have gotten to the spot my dad said was underwater yesterday. I'm not ready to see that.

I park, and Beth practically jumps from the truck, her eyes glued to her phone screen.

"I have bars!" she shouts.

While my passengers make their calls, I get in touch with my older sister, Kristen, who lives in Charlotte with her family. I know my dad already talked to her, but it doesn't hurt to check in again while I have a signal.

"What are the news reports saying, Kris? We're getting no information here."

"Widespread flash flooding and mudslides. Biltmore Village and the River Arts District are underwater. They're refusing to give a body count; it's bad—"

With a long beep, the call drops. I try to call her back, but it won't connect. I try texting instead—letting her know we'll talk to her again when we can—and that goes through.

Looks like Ramona and her friends are having about the same kind of luck. Ramona skulks over to me.

"My phone won't work. It's on a different carrier than Beth's, so I guess that carrier's working better than mine at the moment."

"Do you want to try to text your parents on my phone to let them know you're okay?"

"I already did on Katie's. Beth talked to her husband until the call dropped. She's been calling him back, talking to him as long as she can before the call drops, and then calling again." Ramona laughs. "I hope she'll feel better after this, though. Now that she's talked to him."

"And Katie?"

She rolls her eyes. "Katie won't feel better until we're back in Atlanta. She feels imprisoned here. No offense."

"None taken. Speaking of which, we should try to get some information about the roads."

I hop back in the truck and turn on the radio, scanning through the channels until I find a local NPR affiliate. It's playing regular programming, so I scan through some more, but I can't find any station on AM or FM sharing information about what's going on here in Asheville. My stomach hardens, and I jab the power button with more force than needed.

Climbing back out of the truck, I take Ramona's hand and walk over to a group of people chatting.

"Anyone heard what's going on with the roads?" I ask. "My friends here are from Atlanta and tryin' to get home."

"Everything's closed. I heard I-40 got washed out by mud," one man shares.

"Highway 26, too. Flooding or something. It's closed going down to South Carolina," one of the women adds.

"The only way out right now is 26 up to Tennessee," another woman tells us. "You'd have to go all the way around."

"I heard the airport's open, and there's some flights going out. They said they might close it soon to get supplies in."

"Thanks," I say. "Where did y'all hear that?"

They all mutter about cousins or neighbors or their friends in Alabama. Ramona and I exchange a glance. Alright, then. Not the most trustworthy of sources, but the best we're getting right now.

"I heard Chimney Rock is gone," one of them says as we walk away. I'm not sure if they mean the actual giant rock up in the mountains that's a hiking destination, or the nearby town that's named after it. Either one is possible at this point, I guess.

Katie and Beth are leaning against the truck when we return, apparently finished with their phone calls and texts. Or attempts at phone calls and texts.

"Did you find anything out?" Ramona asks them.

"No," Katie complains. "I couldn't get Jonah on the phone long enough and texts are spotty coming in."

"You?" asks Beth.

"Maybe," I say. I repeat the messages from the grapevine.

Beth frowns. "That's not much to go on."

"Sounds good to me," says Katie. "We should try going up to Tennessee like they said."

Ramona bites her lip. "I don't know, Katie. We don't know how far the effects from this storm go. What if we start driving toward Tennessee, which is way out of our way, and there's nothing open? Or we can't get through? And then we run out of gas and get stranded."

Beth shakes her head. "She's right. We know we're safe here. Let's stay until we have better information."

I let out the breath I'm holding. They *are* safe here, and who knows what conditions are like on the roads. Plus, of course, selfishly, it means I get more time with Ramona.

Katie groans loudly. "I just want to leave!"

Ramona and Beth console their friend, and we load back into the truck and head back to the farm.

I hear Katie grumble to Ramona, "If you move here, you better come visit me, because I'm *never* coming back."

Ramona scoffs. "I'm not moving here."

Ever? I want to ask. Like it's completely out of the question? I hold my tongue because it's way too soon to have that conversation.

Chapter Seven

Kevin

♥

As soon as my feet hit the gravel driveway when I climb out of the truck back at the farm, Beth nudges me and whispers, "It's her birthday."

My eyes go wide. "What?"

"Today is Ramona's thirtieth birthday," she repeats, and she winks. "Thought you might like to know."

"Uh, yeah. Thanks."

Of course, I need to do something, though options are limited right now. What a terrible way for her to spend her birthday.

"Kev!" Ramona calls from the far side of the truck. "We're going to play cards in our cottage. Want to join us?"

On my way past her, I drop a kiss to her forehead and grin. "Yeah ... let me take care of something real quick. I'll meet you there."

I go straight for my cabin and raid the pantry. I don't have much. Truthfully, I'm a bachelor who eats most meals at my parents' house. I don't cook often. I do snack, though. I find a box of chocolate

MoonPies and a plastic platter. I unwrap the pies and arrange them as artistically as I can on the platter—I lay some in a circle for a bottom layer and stagger the next row like bricks on top of the first. I keep going with this pattern until I have a cone of MoonPies six layers high. Oh, wait, a candle. I'm sure I have some. I rifle through the junk drawer until I find a tall taper candle. I take the top Moon-Pie off the stack and eat it. Then, I stick the taper candle in the hole until it's settled on the platter and the wick sticks out the top of the tower.

I step back and examine my work, squinting my eyes. *Okay. So, I made her a birthday volcano.* I shrug. *It'll do.* I shove a lighter in my pocket and walk the platter carefully out the door and across the field to the guest cottage. Katie answers the door, and it's the first time I've seen her smile.

"What is *that*?" she asks gleefully.

"A birthday cake, sort of, for Ramona."

She laughs quietly. "You're an okay guy, Kevin. Other than the fact you live in these stupid mountains."

Katie motions Beth over, and I hear Ramona call out, "What's going on?" The cottage is small, with the door just out of sight of the kitchen table where Ramona must be sitting.

I light the candle, and the three of us walk into the kitchen singing the happy birthday song.

Ramona starts laughing. "Oh my gosh, let me grab my phone so I can take a picture!"

"I've got it!" says Beth and starts recording.

"Nobody's ever made me a birthday ... what is this, exactly?"

I shrug. "Best I can figure is a volcano."

"Nobody's ever made me a birthday volcano out of MoonPies before!"

I set it in front of her, and she blows out the candle.

"Do you like it?" I ask.

Her eyes lock on mine. "I *love* it. Thank you, Kev."

She stands and throws her arms around my neck. I hug her back, relishing her warmth against me. Too soon—for me, though I'm guessing not for our audience—she pulls away.

An awkward beat passes where no one seems to know what to do. So, I rub my hands together and say, "What are we playin'?"

The tension leaks out of the room as the three friends argue about which game to play next. We settle on *Go Fish*, and Ramona deals the cards.

After a few rounds of cards while munching on MoonPies, Beth stands and stretches her back. "I'm going to take a walk."

Katie looks between Beth and Ramona. "I'll go with you."

"Be good you two!" they sing-song as they head out the door.

I grin and shake my head. "More *Go Fish*?" I ask. "Or maybe *Memory*?"

"Yeah, let's play *Memory*." Ramona's eyes go hazy as I line up the cards in as even of rows as I can on the small table.

"I have season tickets to the Braves," she blurts.

I repeat her words slowly. "You have season tickets to the Braves."

"Well *one* season ticket."

I'm staring at her trying to figure out if this means what I think it means. Her cheeks turn pink as I study her. "Why?"

"We always talked about going to a game together, but we never did, so I went by myself that summer after you graduated. Well, with friends. And I loved it, so I kept going back. I started buying a season ticket a couple years ago. At first it was ... I wanted to feel close to you." She drops her eyes. "I missed you."

My throat constricts with emotion. All these years I couldn't stop thinking about her. I couldn't shake her no matter how hard I tried. Could it be she felt the same about me?

"I missed you, too," I murmur. "So much." I chuckle dryly. "I mean, I've been naming all my damn horses after movies I watched with you. Trying to keep you close."

Her eyes widen. "Then why ... I know in the end we both agreed to go our separate ways. I was still in school in Atlanta, and you were coming back home to North Carolina. We didn't want to do the long-distance thing. But if you missed me so much, why did you stop texting?"

It's my turn to be surprised. "I didn't. No ... you're the one who stopped texting me."

We lock eyes, and both start laughing.

"What happened?" Ramona wonders. She goes still and then gasps. "I ... dropped my phone in the pool that summer," she says carefully. "I had to get a new one. It was the same number and everything, but for weeks after I'd get random texts with no contact name or conversation history. If you texted me—"

"I did," I interrupt.

"—I might not have realized it was you." She groans. "All these years I thought ... Wait, if I meant so much to you why didn't you want to be my official boyfriend?"

I splutter. "I did. More than anything. I thought we agreed mutually to keep it casual. I didn't want to pressure you, especially since I knew I'd be graduating and leaving. Is that what you thought all this time? That I didn't want you as my girlfriend? Ramona, it's *all* I wanted."

She sits quietly, absorbing this information. "Well," she finally says, "apparently our twenty-year-old selves weren't very good at communicating."

"Apparently."

We both stare at the cards lined up on the table.

"I wonder what could have..." she says, her soft voice trailing off at the end.

"Yeah," I say thickly. Maybe we would have been married by now. A couple kids even. But where? This farm, my family's legacy, is everything to me—and her life is in Atlanta. Always has been. Maybe those barriers are too much.

***

After a dinner of spaghetti and green beans with my family, I walk outside with Ramona.

Clearing my throat, I ask, "Would you want to see my cabin?" It's not a line—I'm not trying to make a move or anything—I'd just like her to see it.

She smirks. "Your cabin, huh?"

My face flushes. "I didn't mean—"

Laughing, she rests a hand on my arm. "I know. I'd love to see your house."

I take her hand, and we walk across the field to my cabin. I push open the door—I never lock it except before I go to bed at night—and usher her inside. The shadows are getting dark in the dusky evening, so I grab a lantern from the side table where I left it last night and pop it open.

As the light illuminates the open concept living room and kitchen, I try to see the cabin through Ramona's eyes. My cabin is slightly bigger than the guest cottage. The living room is more spacious, it can fit a full sectional sofa instead of the love seat in the cottage. Across from the sofa is a giant TV, useless now. The kitchen is considerably larger—a full kitchen rather than a kitchenette. Not that I use it for more than brewing coffee and heating up leftovers.

I lead her down a hallway like the one in the cottage that leads to two bedrooms. My bedroom has an ensuite bathroom, while the bedroom across the hall—which I use for an office and gaming room—does not. There's a full bathroom at the end of the hall for guests. I haven't decorated. My sister bought me a few throw pillows and framed art prints. Still, the dark oak furniture looks stark against the mostly bare walls. My mom nags me about making my place look homier, but no one comes over, and I'm usually outside, in the barn, or at my parents' house. Now, though, with Ramona surveying the place, I wish I had put in more effort.

I watch her uneasily, not sure why I'm so invested in her opinion of my cabin.

Finally, she says, "This place is as bland as your college apartment was. But it's cute. It has good bones. It's bigger than it seems from outside."

My lips quirk up. "Thanks."

We stand staring at each other for a few seconds before I remember my manners. "Have a seat. Can I get you warm bottled water or a warm can of soda?"

She laughs. "Water would be great. It would be better if you had ice."

"No ice. Sorry."

"Yeah." She sighs.

"What do you want to do? Your choice, birthday girl." I set our bottles of water on the coffee table and sit on the sofa as close to her as I can.

She shoves my shoulder. "I can guess what you'd like to do."

I hope she can't, because I'm sure her guess is much tamer than my thoughts. I shrug carelessly.

"It's your birthday, so you decide."

"Oh, goody. Once a year I get to decide what we do?" Her sarcastic tone is funny; her words telling. Is she thinking of us together beyond this trip? Is there a future reality where the two of us are deciding what to do together on a regular basis? I let the mounting questions slide away and grin.

"You can choose what we do whenever you want, baby." Especially if what she wants to do is make out.

Her eyes light up with an idea and then dim again.

"What?" I ask.

"I had an idea, but—"

"But nothin'. Let's hear it."

"We can read out loud to each other." She blushes. "Stupid, right?"

"Of course it's not stupid. I'm not sure what books I have around. I don't usually have much time for reading."

She pulls her phone from her pocket. "I have e-books on my phone. My battery is doing pretty well, thanks to those power banks you lent us."

"Okay, let's read." I know I said she could choose, but I don't love this plan. "What's the book?"

She scrolls through her phone and then taps the screen. "Oh, this is perfect. It's a novella, which means it's short. *And* the chapters are alternating points of view, so we can trade off reading." Her eyes sparkle, which tells me there's more to this perfect book.

"What?" I ask her.

She grins. "It's a romance."

I groan. "Come on, baby."

"It's a clean romance, so don't worry about any, you know, uncomfortable scenes."

She looks so proud of herself and so adorable sitting on my sofa clutching her phone to her chest, that I'd give her anything she asked for at this moment. Hell, I'd give her anything she asked for forever.

I lean back on the couch and pull her onto my lap. I press a kiss to the top of her head and move my lips right next to her ear. "As you wish."

The quote's from one of *my* favorite movies, *The Princess Bride*. It's one I introduced her to in college. See, I know romance.

I feel her shiver in my arms, and I pull her tighter against me.

"Okay, let's see this romance book."

She turns her attention back to her phone screen, clears her throat, and says, "Chapter one."

Chapter Eight

Ramona

♥

My birthday yesterday ended up being a surprisingly great day. It started rough when we couldn't get the information we needed to make a decision about driving home. Then Kevin made me a MoonPie cake volcano thing, and we hung out and talked. Really talked, like we've needed to for a while. I can't believe all this time it was probably my phone's fault I stopped hearing from Kevin. I should have texted him when I stopped getting his texts. If not for my stupid pride, where would we be now?

We finished off the night reading to each other. It was just as cheesy and romantic as it sounds. Kevin put effort into reading his parts and actually seemed to enjoy the story.

I know all this has an expiration date. As soon as we know it's safe, my friends and I will drive home to Atlanta, and then what? As much as I wish it could be more, this time with Kevin can only be a stolen interlude, bittersweet closure for our long-ago relationship.

If only he didn't affect me as much now as he always did. If only I didn't feel, impossibly, like I've already fallen for him again.

When the three of us are all up and dressed, having sponge-bathed with wet wipes and shared Beth's can of dry shampoo, we go find Kevin in the barn again.

Like yesterday—Saturday, was it?—he's taking care of the horses. We're here earlier today, so we catch him in the middle of cleaning out the stalls. Though the outside air has a fall chill to it, the barn is warm, and Kevin's dressed in jeans and a short-sleeve t-shirt. With each scoop of the shovel, his biceps flex and pull against his sleeves. I think about how those muscles felt underneath my hands while we cuddled on his couch the night before—firm and solid. Strong.

He looks up and notices me, his eyes lighting up. "Mornin', baby!"

I've always found it cringey when men call women "baby." It's degrading and cheesy. When *Kevin* calls *me* "baby," though, with a slight twang on the first syllable, I get lightheaded and have to fight the urge to giggle.

"And good morning, ladies," he adds, tilting his chin toward Beth and Katie.

"Good morning, Kevin," Beth calls out, standing back from the horse stalls.

"Hey," says Katie, "we're going to the magical parking lot again to see if we can get better information. Are you coming or not?"

Kevin grins at that. "Yeah, I'll drive you. Give me a minute to finish here and clean up?"

"We'll meet you at your truck."

We've developed a routine, almost, in only a couple of days. And judging by a lack of progress on the basic utilities and communication front, we might be continuing this routine for several days yet.

***

When we pull into a parking space behind McDonald's, my phone instantly starts pinging with notifications. It's a glorious sound. I look in the top right corner of my phone screen and see I have a data connection. Social media messages, text messages, and a couple of voicemails come through. I feel so silly when actual tears come to my eyes.

We get out of the truck to see if we can boost the signal more. Kevin starts searching for news information, while Katie opens the maps app on her phone. Beth calls her husband and is talking to her kids.

The connection isn't perfect. Pages and apps take forever to load and tend to freeze if there's too much content. Still, I'm able to get to a web page that tracks highway closures in North Carolina. I've learned there are two major highways going through Asheville. I-40 goes east and west, and I-26 goes north and south. On the drive here, we mostly took smaller US highways from Atlanta until we got on I-40 just west of Asheville. Today, I-40 going in either direction is closed. If we'd listened to the lady yesterday who said to take 26 up to Tennessee, we'd have been in trouble, because that route is also closed.

"26 south!" Katie yells, and we all turn to stare at her. She lowers her voice and repeats. "Looks like 26 south is open. I can't get everything to load though." She swipes at her screen a few more times before she groans in frustration. "It's not loading at all anymore."

Seems the magic is gone for our phones, too, because the page I'm on freezes. Kevin's too, I'm guessing, since he slips it into his pocket.

"I'm going to ask around," he says. "Maybe someone has better information."

Beth finishes her phone call. "How's everyone doing?" I ask her.

Beth takes a deep breath and lets it out. "Fine. Dan seems to have things under control."

Kevin comes back and says, "Good news. The home improvement store down the road is open and has their Wi-Fi working. We can go in the store and get a more reliable signal."

"Sounds like a plan," says Katie, already opening the truck door to get back in. "Let's go."

With the stable Wi-Fi connection in the store, we confirm we can drive south on 26 and catch Highway 20 west in Columbia, South Carolina to get home (a roundabout way to go, but we don't want to chance smaller roads being blocked). I also ask a police officer standing outside the store, who verifies 26 south is indeed open.

"Remember," Beth says. "We have about one hundred miles of gas in the SUV. How far will that get us?"

Kevin flips his hat around on his head. "Spartanburg is about seventy miles down 26. That's probably your best bet. It's large enough, and hopefully far away enough, that they'll have power and gas."

"Okay," I say. "Sounds like we have a plan. Let's get back to the farm and pack up." I catch and hold Kevin's gaze, and he shoots me a smile that doesn't make it all the way to his eyes.

I know we need to get home. Beth's family needs her. Katie's driving everyone crazy. All three of us are supposed to be at work tomorrow. Besides, the longer we stay, the more of a burden we are on Kevin and his family. They need their supplies for themselves, especially when it's unclear when services will return to normal or more supplies will come in.

But—

I don't want to leave Kevin. I can't see how the feelings we have for each other, again, even after only a couple of days, can survive with him here and me back home in Atlanta. It's not sustainable. Is it? Even if we make it work in the short term, what about in the long term? Eventually someone will have to move, or we'll have to break up. By that point, we'll be so much more invested, and it will hurt so much more.

***

As we're packing our bags, I hear a knock on the cottage door. I open it to see Kevin and greet him with a smile.

"Hey!"

His face is smooth, expressionless. "Can I talk to you a minute, please?"

My heart starts pounding. Are we doing this now? He's going to say of course there's no reason to prolong this little fling we've been having. It's what I think, too, and yet I hoped maybe he'd disagree with me, try to make me change my mind. Dread pools in my stomach.

"Sure." I step out onto the porch, and we walk around the corner, out of sight of the cottage windows.

He doesn't say anything at first, so I give him an expectant look. He's standing with his feet spread in line with his hips. His arms are crossed in front of him, his hands in fists. His lips are pressed together, and his eyebrows knitted on his forehead. He should maybe seem intimidating, standing before me like a brick wall of a man. Instead, I'm awash with feelings of safety and protection.

"Everything okay?" I prompt. I'd like to get this over with.

"I'm going with you." His voice is steely, as if he's expecting an argument he won't entertain.

"What do you mean?" I'm half-confused and half-hopeful. He's coming with me to load the car? He's coming with me to Atlanta to be with me forever? He needs to be more specific.

"I'm concerned you'll run out of gas and be stranded. I'd like to follow in my truck at least until you find gas."

I tilt my head at him, and his face softens. Easing his rigid posture, he puts his hands on my shoulders and slides them over my arms.

"I want to make sure you're safe," he says quietly. "That you can get out safely. We still don't know exactly what the extent of the damage is around here, or how far out it stretches. If I follow in my truck, I'll be there if you need help."

For the second time this morning, I blink back tears. "How much gas do *you* have?"

"Almost a full tank. I filled up Thursday on my way home. And I'll bring our empty gas cans so I can buy more when we find someplace open."

"Okay," I tell him.

"Okay? You're not going to argue with me?"

I shake my head. "I do have one condition."

He narrows his eyes. "What is it?"

"I ride in the truck with you until you turn back."

Kevin grins, relaxing fully now. "Done."

Chapter Nine

Ramona

♥

As our caravan makes its way toward I-26, Kevin finally finds a local radio station talking uninterrupted about what's going on in western North Carolina. Listeners call in trying to contact loved ones in remote mountain towns or to ask about the status of the nursing home their grandmother is in. One man calls and says his wife is out of oxygen and if anyone knows how he can get another tank, he'd be grateful. Within ten minutes, the host reports back that he's had calls from people willing to donate an oxygen tank and brave the roads to get it to the man and his wife.

Meanwhile, it takes us forty minutes to get to 26; a trip that can normally be made in fifteen, Kevin tells me. There are cars on the road and navigating through large intersections without streetlights is tricky. Plus, on the smaller roads, we're literally driving over, un- der, and around power lines and tree branches. In several spots, only one lane is open and the vehicles heading in either direction take turns edging around the large trees that have yet to be moved from the other travel lane.

Despite these clues, it's not until we're out of the mountains far enough that I can consistently use my phone that I realize how devastating the situation is in Asheville and the surrounding areas. Even with the inconveniences and anxiety of the last few days, we've been in a bubble on Kevin's family property. Downed trees and power lines are the least of western North Carolina's worries. As I scroll through video after video of the destruction from flash flooding and mudslides, my heart heaves.

"Kev," I say quietly. "Biltmore Village is completely underwater."

He glances at me quickly before turning his eyes back to the road. My eyes are glued to my phone where videos show brown, muddy water rushing around and through houses and cars. Some of the more remote mountain towns are completely gone. People washed away in the flood waters with their homes. More are still missing. It's hard to stomach.

I think about the places I've been and people I've met in North Carolina this week. The tour guide at the chocolate factory. The hikers we passed on the trail. Even the woman in the gold dress that first night at the bookstore. What are their lives like now? Do they still have jobs, homes, families?

I set my phone face down in my lap, close my eyes, and rest the back of my head against the seat. I feel Kevin's hand on my thigh, squeezing. The pain of the devastation here and the anticipation of leaving Kevin, plus echoes of the long-ago pain of missing Kevin after he graduated swirl together in my belly. Without opening my eyes, I move my hand to his and interlace our fingers.

***

As we drive out of the mountains and cross into South Carolina, I call Katie in the car behind us and stay on the line with her so we can decide where to stop. So far, there aren't many exits that look like they have electricity, let alone open gas stations.

"How's your gas looking?" I ask Katie.

"Uhh, still forty miles. We're doing okay."

We decide to investigate the Spartanburg exits. At the first one, Kevin turns right, and we see gas stations. We look closer, and they're all without power and closed. He turns the truck around to get back on the interstate.

I stretch my neck to see out the front windshield better. "Wait! That looks like an open gas station there."

I point to a sign in the distance lit up, advertising the price per gallon. I'm still on the phone with Katie, so I tell her, and she sees it too. As we get closer, we notice a long line of cars on a side street.

"Bet you anything they're all in line for gas," Katie says over the phone line.

"Oh, without a doubt."

Kevin looks at me. "What do you want to do?"

"We need to get in line. Right?"

Katie agrees, and I hear Beth in the background saying, "Thirty miles until empty. We might as well wait in line here. I doubt things will be better ten or twenty miles up the road."

Kevin turns right and joins the line. Beth and Katie pull up behind us.

"I'm going to hang up now," I tell Katie.

Katie laughs. "Should we play the 'you hang up first' game?"

I groan. "I don't think that's necessary. But I'm glad you seem to be feeling better already."

She's already hung up. I laugh and shake my head. The next thing I know, there's a knock on my window, and I nearly jump out of my skin. It's Katie. I put the window down and raise my eyebrows at her.

"I'm going to walk to the front of the line to see what the situation is. Like are they taking cash only, how much gas do they have, things like that."

"Sounds good," I say. "We'll be here."

Katie salutes and walks away, following the line of cars on foot. I put the window back up and look over at Kevin, who's staring at his phone, getting sucked into the photos and videos of the destruction, just like I did.

I put my hand on his arm. "You'll drive yourself crazy with all that."

Lifting his eyes, he shakes his head. "This is so much worse than I thought. Than anyone thought. We weren't prepared for any of it. There were no warnings or anything. We thought it would just be a rainy, windy night."

I don't know what to say. This is his home. As emotional as I feel seeing the destruction, he must feel it ten times worse. After all, I get to leave and go home to my safe, comfortable apartment with electricity and water.

Maybe I can ease his burden. Let him off the hook as far as any kind of expectations from me are concerned. I can feign indifference if it makes things easier for him.

My heart thudding, I broach the subject. "Listen, as far as, um, I don't know, anything with me and you going forward ... you know, since I'm going home to Atlanta and you're dealing with recovery efforts here..."

Kevin's eyes, an intense steely blue, snap up to mine, and I trail off. He doesn't say anything, just keeps watching me. So, I bumble on.

"Um, no pressure. It could be just a fun couple of days. This doesn't need to go anywhere or be anything serious."

He stares at me for so long that I have to tell him when the line starts moving again. He shifts his eyes back to the road.

"You're fooling yourself. Baby, you and me were made for serious. And at this point in my life, I'm not interested in anything less. Especially not with you."

Now it's my turn to stare. He *wants* to be serious? I love that he wants to be serious; I'm not sure how it will work.

We're interrupted by Katie knocking at the window again. I open it to talk to her.

"The line's long. They have plenty of gas though, they said. It's card only. No cash. It looks like they're running the whole station from a huge generator. And there's a store they operate, too. Kevin, they have cases of bottled water and stuff if you want to bring some back."

Kevin rubs his chin. "Yeah, that's a good idea. I'll stock up while I can."

Katie returns to Beth's SUV as the line of cars inches steadily forward. Kevin hasn't said anything else, so I don't either. The truck is quiet the rest of the way to the gas station.

We finally reach the front of the line and pull up to a gas pump. Kevin fills the truck first, and then each of his gas cans. On the opposite side of the pump from us, Beth is filling her SUV. She gives me a thumbs up, and I let out a breath. We should have plenty of gas to get home now, even going the long way around.

Kevin signals Beth. "I'll meet you in the parking lot over there so you can get your final passenger."

She flashes him a thumbs up, then finishes filling her tank before Kevin gets all the gas cans full. Meanwhile, I sit anxiously in the cab of the truck. Are we going to talk more? Everything feels unsettled, my palms are clammy. I spent two days kissing and talking to Kevin King, and I'm already more than halfway to being as in love with him as ever. Which, ultimately, means heartbreak. If not today, eventually.

Kevin's still quiet when he climbs back into the driver seat and navigates to a nearby parking lot where Beth and Katie are waiting for me. He stops a row over from them, shuts off the truck, and smooths his hands over the jeans covering his thighs. He still doesn't say anything, so, fighting back tears, I open my door and jump down.

My suitcase is already in the SUV, so all I need to do is walk over, get in, drive away, and apparently never see Kevin King again. It's better that way, anyway. Isn't it?

In a flash, Kevin is out of the truck and rounding the hood until he stands in front of me. He puts his hands against my cheeks, then slides them to my arms, and finally my hands, where he intertwines our fingers.

"I know you have to go," he says gruffly. "I don't want this to be goodbye."

"What *do* you want?" I whisper. I'm losing the battle against my tears, and they begin trickling down my face. He lets go of one of my hands to wipe my cheeks with his thumb, the callouses rough against my skin.

"I want you."

"Kevin, we still have the same problem as nine years ago. Your life is here and mine is in Atlanta. How can it work? Nothing has changed."

Kevin considers my words for a moment, then carefully says, "*We've* changed. We're not kids anymore. We have a better idea now of what we want and what else is out there. And Ramona, I can tell you there is no one out there I'd rather be with than you."

It's too perfect of a line, and what's more, I think he genuinely means it. Sucker that I've always been for him, I eat it up with a spoon. There's no way I can turn him down, even if I'll regret it later. I look away from his eyes, hoping to break the spell. But even when I shift my gaze over his shoulder, all I want is to be wrapped in his arms.

I notice Katie and Beth leaning against the SUV and not even pretending they aren't watching our every move.

"Kevin..." I say and shrug. I can't stop the corners of my lips from turning up into a smile. He lights me up. Always has.

"All I know is I'm not making the same mistake again. I'm not letting you walk away without a commitment."

"A ... commitment?" I feel my eyebrows scrunch together.

He grins, then kneels in front of me, holding one hand against his heart, and keeping the other wrapped up in my fingers. Katie gasps. My brain tells me to take a step back as my body leans in.

"Ramona Carpenter, will you be my girlfriend?"

I laugh and pull his arm until he's on his feet. "You're an idiot." I roll my eyes. "Yes, I will."

An uneasiness rises in my stomach. Questions about how any of this can work long term flood my mind; I push them away. I want this too badly. I'll ignore logic and sense for now and get swept up in the romance. I know in the depths of my soul this is going to hurt later. A lot. I can't seem to make myself care at the moment. That's a problem for tomorrow Ramona. Today Ramona kisses Kevin an indecent amount of time before Katie and Beth make exaggerated throat-clearing noises and we pull apart.

It's goodbye for now.

Chapter Ten

I wake with a start, images of muddy, rushing water still flashing through my thoughts. I rub my eyes and grapple to find my cell phone on the nightstand. Three in the morning. Again. I've been having these nightmares every night this week since I've been home. Nightmares of the horror in North Carolina that I've only ever seen in videos online, interspersed with faces of the people I met there. How am I so affected by these disasters when I didn't experience them, not really? I have no right to complain, no right to be haunted when I'm safe and clean and dry in my bed in Atlanta.

I have the strongest yearning to talk to Kevin. Of course it's impossible. Even if I could get him on a call for more than a few minutes without the signal dropping, how can I complain to him about what I'm feeling when he's still there living it? When his whole community has been devastated. It's just selfish.

I toss and turn for a few more hours before giving up. I climb out of bed and start getting ready for work, rubbing the sides of my jaw, sore near the joints. I've been clenching my teeth in my sleep, leaving me tired and my head aching.

When I get out of the shower, I have a text waiting for me from Kevin.

Kevin:
Mornin baby

Ramona:
Good morning

Kevin:
Send me another picture, please. I want to see your beautiful face

Thanks to mini cell phone towers set up around the area after the storm went through, Kevin and I have been able to text consistently, even sending photos. Phone calls are still spotty.

I get dressed and do my hair and makeup before I snap a selfie and text it to Kevin.

Ramona:
Now you [wink face emoji]

Kevin:
You look beautiful this morning

He texts me a picture of himself, and I can tell he's in the barn. He doesn't have his hat on, and his hair is mussed. His eyes look tired above his smiling lips. Handsome as always. I text him a string of hearts in response.

Ramona:

I miss you

Kevin:

I miss you too baby

My mind drifts to the nightmare I had again last night. Kevin and his family still have no electricity—other than the generator—and no running water. And it's worse for so many others. It feels wrong to be living my normal life with all the suffering happening a few hours to the north.

Between my stress reactions post-Asheville and missing Kevin an embarrassing amount considering we've only just started dating again, I have to drag myself to the car to drive to work.

When I get to the office, I stop in the break room for extra coffee. As I'm stirring in the cream, a word from the conversation two coworkers are having on the other side of the room grabs my attention—Asheville. I lean my ear closer so I can hear better, only catching the last phrase as they walk out the door: "... wish there was something I could do to help."

Me too, I think. They need so many supplies up there to get them through. Supplies that are scarce right now in North Carolina but plentiful here in Georgia. An obvious idea leaps through my thoughts, and I stop stirring my coffee as I latch onto the idea and turn it over in my mind.

What if I collected a bunch of supplies and drove them up to Asheville for Kevin, his family, and their neighbors?

I nurse the idea all the way through lunch, considering logistics. Finally in the afternoon I call Beth.

"Would Dan lend me his truck?" I ask.

"For what?"

I explain my idea to her, saying I want to drive the truck up to Asheville this weekend to deliver supplies—and see Kevin of course.

"It's a brilliant idea," Beth says. "No, I don't think Dan would lend you his truck."

My heart sinks. Maybe I can rent a truck, or—

"I bet he'd drive up there with you. We could get Jonah to go. I'll have to stay with the kids, but you might be able to convince Katie."

I laugh. "I doubt it, but the rest sounds great!"

A few texts to the group chat later and my friends have all agreed to collect supplies at their respective workplaces. Katie decidedly will *not* come with us. Dan and Jonah are in. I get permission from my boss to email our immediate department to ask for donations.

I feel lighter than I have in weeks. I get to see Kevin this weekend, and I'm putting my energy into a project that matters and I'm excited about. Too bad it's not for my job.

My main project for work right now is assisting on a campaign to advertise champagne that retails at $1,000 a bottle. The marketing campaign centers on an expensive Super Bowl commercial with taglines and smaller pieces branching off that. No shade to anyone who enjoys a nice glass of champagne occasionally—I know I do—but such a luxury feels pointless, and even callous, in the wake of the disaster in North Carolina.

In the evening, I call Kevin. I want to hear his voice when I explain my plan, so I hope the service holds out.

He picks up right away, his characteristic grin evident in his words as he says, "Hey, baby."

Instantly, my heart feels lighter, even as it beats more quickly. I can't stop the smile that overtakes my face when I hear his voice, nor can I stop the tears welling up in my eyes. Good thing this isn't a video call. I blink them back and make sure my voice is steady before responding.

"Hi."

"I love hearing your voice. How was your day today?"

"Actually, that's why I'm calling. I had an idea..." I explain my plan to him, including Dan, Jonah, and me driving up this weekend with whatever supplies we collect. "We'd come up on Saturday and stay overnight, leaving Sunday. So, it would be a short visit," I finish.

The line is quiet. Maybe the call dropped?

"Kev? Are you still there?"

"Yeah. Sorry ... I just ... baby, that's amazing. You're amazing." His voice is rough. "I would love to see you this weekend. And meet Dan and Jonah. And accept the supplies and get them distributed to our neighbors. And I would love to see you this weekend."

I laugh. "You already said that."

"Well, it's my favorite part of the whole plan."

Mine, too.

***

Kevin's grinning broadly as he watches us pull up in the truck.

"Baby, guess what?" he greets me, calling out as soon as my head peeks out from the truck.

"What?" I grin back as I reach the ground and walk toward him.

"I took a real shower today!"

I step back. "You did? Is the water back on?"

"No, I went to one of those mobile shower stations."

With one of the two major water treatment plants still out of commission, the county government has set up community care stations throughout the area with access to showers, laundry facilities, cell towers and Wi-Fi, hot meals, and counseling services. They're using water from tankers they've trucked in from outside Asheville.

I'm close enough to Kevin now that he grabs me around the waist and pulls me into him, wrapping me tightly in his arms. I take a deep breath through my nose, reveling in his clean, soapy scent.

"I wanted to be able to do this without scaring you away," he murmurs into my hair.

I laugh. "I appreciate that."

Honestly, the idea of him planning ahead, finding a mobile shower station, going there, standing in a strange shower, is overwhelmingly touching. I breathe deeply and snuggle closer into his soft hoodie.

Dan clears his throat, and I try to step away from Kevin, but he keeps me tucked against his side as he extends a hand to Dan and then Jonah.

"Hey man, what's up. I'm Kevin. Thank y'all so much for driving up here."

"Sorry," I break in. "Kevin, this is Dan, Beth's husband, and Jonah, Katie's fiancé."

The guys greet each other, and Kevin's eyes twinkle. "Katie didn't want to come?" he asks Jonah with a smile.

Jonah scoffs. "Man, I couldn't have dragged her here. She says she's never going to the mountains ever again. It's a good thing I planned a tropical vacation for our honeymoon."

We all laugh and then show Kevin what we brought: cases of bottled water, nonperishable food, fresh fruits and vegetables, cleaning wipes, batteries, a couple of small propane stoves, bags of charcoal, and several cans of gasoline. What Kevin and his family and neighbors can't use, they'll distribute to others in need.

"Here, let me show y'all to your rooms."

Kevin leads the way to the cottage, still holding me against his side. We decided earlier in the week that the guys would sleep here, and I'd sleep in Kevin's cabin. Not like *that*. I'll be in Kevin's bed, and he said he'll either set up an air mattress in the game room, or sleep on the couch. One issue is sheets. Of course, Kevin hasn't been able to do laundry. There are a few mobile laundry stations set up around the area. Apparently, they're serving so many people that they have to limit to two loads each, so obviously clothing has been the priority. Though Kevin says his family has a few extra sets of sheets, I feel bad dirtying them for one night when Kevin and his family might need them for themselves. As a compromise, we brought our own sleeping bags and pillows, plus I bought a couple of new sets of sheets to give to the Kings.

Kevin gives Dan and Jonah a quick tour, making sure they know protocol for flushing the toilet. He's restless, rushing through the instructions. After a few minutes, he gestures at the door.

"I'd like to hang around and get to know you two better, but—"

Jonah laughs. "But you'd rather spend time with Ramona?" He puts his hands up as if to ward off Kevin's protests. "It's cool, man. If I hadn't seen my girlfriend in two weeks, I'd be *much* more eager to hang out with her than with two ugly guys like us."

Dan puts out his hand to shake Kevin's again. "Yeah, man, no worries. You won't hurt our feelings. We just want to help. Let us know if there's anything we can do while we're here." He snaps his fingers. "As a matter of fact, we can start by unloading the truck. Where do you want everything?"

Kevin shows them the storage area off the porch of his parents' house and introduces them to his mom, dad, and aunt. He makes a half-hearted offer to help unload, but the guys hand him my suitcase and practically shove us out the door.

"We'll take care of the boys here," Kevin's mom calls. "You take care of Ramona."

I feel my cheeks warm. I *really* hope no one gets the wrong idea. I know Kevin's on the same page—we talked about expectations and boundaries a couple of days ago before I drove up. I can guess the assumptions his family are making, though. While I fully expect to be kissing and cuddling while I'm here, I'm not looking for more until we get to know each other again.

We're just inside the door of Kevin's cabin when he gently sets down my suitcase and, not so gently, pushes me against the closed door and kisses me intently. I wrap my arms around his neck and return the favor. After a few minutes, I pull back.

"Hi," I say breathlessly.

He gives me a lopsided smile. "Hey. I missed you."

My heart squeezes. "I missed you, too."

With my back still against the door, I rest my head on his chest. He kisses my temple.

"I guess we should get you settled," he says against my hair.

"I feel pretty settled right here."

He squeezes me. "I'm glad."

I sigh. "But, yeah, you're right. I'll put my bag away."

In Kevin's room, I put my suitcase on the bed and unzip it.

"You're only here one night," Kevin reminds me. "Why do you need a whole suitcase? I mean, unless you're planning to stay longer. That'd be fine with me." He grins hopefully.

I shake my head and hide a smile. "No, just tonight. Be nice, because I brought my big suitcase so I could pack your presents."

Kevin rubs his hands together. "Presents?"

"Yup." I hand him the sheets. "New sheets, and not only because I worried I'd have to sleep on your stinky ones."

He laughs.

I pull out a large paper grocery bag. "We brought all sorts of nonperishable food and snacks for everyone of course; these are for your personal stash."

He sets the packages of sheets on the bed next to the suitcase and reaches for the bag, his eyes alight. *Like a kid on Christmas*, I think.

He laughs when the first food he pulls out is a block of cheddar cheese.

"I checked and hard cheeses do not need to be refrigerated. You need to eat it quicker though when it's not."

He shakes his head and pulls out the next item—a box of butter crackers.

He slowly releases a breath and steps closer. "You remembered."

Cheese and crackers were our go-to when we studied together back in college. Kevin always said it was the perfect salty snack.

"Of course I did."

His eyes are fixed on mine. "Okay, I have to kiss you again."

I smirk. "Oh, yeah?"

"Definitely."

Chapter Eleven

Kevin

♥

I wake up in the middle of the night, which is unusual for me. Checking my phone, I see it's about three in the morning. I lie in the dark for a few minutes trying to figure out what woke me. Then I hear soft whimpering sounds coming from down the hall where Ramona's sleeping in my bedroom. I practically leap from the couch and toward the closed door. I knock softly once, and let myself in.

She's having a nightmare. Still asleep, her body shifts back and forth on the bed. She's making these mewling sounds that break my heart. I kneel on the floor next to the bed and smooth her hair from her face.

I rub her back and whisper, "Baby. Baby, wake up. You're having a bad dream."

She stills and slowly opens her eyes. "Kev?"

"Yeah, baby. I'm here. You were having a bad dream."

She presses her eyes closed, then opens them and fixes them on me. She looks weary. And not because she's awake and it's the middle of the night. She looks world-weary, haunted—like this isn't the first or second time something like this has happened.

She reaches up and strokes my cheek, and my eyes flutter closed. "Thanks," she murmurs.

"Anytime. Are you okay?"

She shifts over in the bed and tugs my hand, so I lie next to her on my side, our faces inches apart.

She yawns. "Get under the covers."

I swallow. "I don't think that's a good idea." Not when she's only here for one night and woke up after a nightmare. I'm trying to be a gentleman here.

She must like to torture me, though.

"'Kay," she says sleepily as she moves her hand to my head and runs her fingers through my hair. She drops it to my shoulder, touching my bare skin.

She cracks an eye open. "You're not wearing a shirt."

"Uh, no. I ... I don't usually sleep with a shirt on." The only reason I'm wearing gym shorts is because Ramona is here. I ... think? It's getting hard to concentrate on anything other than her fingers moving lightly over my shoulder and biceps.

"I don't mind," she says. Her eyes are closing again, and the crease that forms between her eyebrows reminds me to focus. I shake my head to clear my thoughts.

"Baby, you were having a nightmare. Do you want to talk about it?"

"Hmm?" With her eyes still closed, she winces. She blinks them open and homes in on my face. "I've been having them for the last couple of weeks."

Weeks? "Like since you went home?"

I see her nod through the darkness. "They're about the flood waters. From the videos."

The flood waters from the videos...

"Baby, are you having nightmares about Asheville?" I find her hand and link our fingers together, pressing both our hands against my chest.

She sighs. "Sort of. It's not anything I experienced myself. I've been feeling ... kind of stressed or something about what happened here. I know I shouldn't—"

I furrow my forehead. "Why shouldn't you?"

"Because I left and went home where I can do things like, you know, take a shower and do laundry. Nothing happened to me or my home or my family or job. I don't have any right to be distressed. I didn't ... I didn't earn it."

I quietly absorb her words. Does she feel guilty this natural disaster happened to us and not to her? It *did* happen to her. She was here, same as I was. And yeah, she went home, but of course she did.

"No one expected you to stay and suffer here with us. And no one blames you for it either."

"No, I know. I'm just ... just being selfish, I think."

"You, selfish? Hardly. You collected all those supplies, and now you're spending your weekend delivering them to us. That's not something a selfish person does."

I can feel more than see the tears rolling down her face. She sniffles, and her voice is thick when she says, "I'm having trouble seeing what the point is. Like, why does anything I'm doing matter? I sit at work and think, how can anyone care about selling more stupid stuff to millionaires when people up here are still looking for their family members? When people's homes are completely gone. When they've lost everything. I thought coming back would help; it's just reminding me again."

I wrap my arm around her back and pull her body into mine. As she sobs against my chest, I kiss her hair and hold her. I blink back tears of my own. For my city of Asheville and my home in North Carolina, and for Ramona's tender heart and empathetic spirit, for the pain she's experiencing.

***

We must fall asleep at some point, because the next thing I know I wake up in my bed, the morning sun streaming through the window of my bedroom. I worked my way under the covers sometime in my sleep, and Ramona and I are tangled together, her head resting on my shoulder like a pillow.

Her lips are pouted out in her sleep, and a line of freckles are spread across her gorgeous face. Her hair's a mess—wild and knotted where it rests against my arm. Her skin is still puffy around her eyes from the crying she did last night—or, rather, early this morning. She's beautiful. Fragile and strong, simultaneously. Both independent and needy, bold and shy.

I love her.

Maybe that's crazy to think considering I've spent a grand total of four days with her in nearly a decade. I loved her in college, too, and spent way more time with her then. I've loved her all this time. The feelings were simmering beneath the surface of my heart, keeping it off-limits to anyone else. It's always been hers, my heart. And, sure, we've both changed through the years, but not in the essential ways, not in who we are at our cores. We still fit, like two pieces of a puzzle.

Ramona stirs in my arms, blinking awake. She smiles and kisses the underside of my chin, so I pull her tighter, trying to imprint the smell of her hair on my psyche. So much has sucked about the last two weeks. There have been so many difficult and emotional problems to solve and so many tragic stories to absorb. But this—this is a moment of perfect happiness. A core memory I'll carry with me throughout the rest of my life, no matter what happens next.

"Good morning," she says against my neck. Her breath against my skin makes me shiver.

"Mornin'," I reply, pressing a kiss to the top of her head.

I expect her to be shy after crying in my arms last night, maybe feel embarrassed. Instead, she's confident and assured, as if her vulnerability has connected us more securely to each other. Like I passed some sort of test and earned her trust more fully.

I'll take it. I don't have any intention of betraying that trust. I'll do whatever it takes to keep her in my life this time around.

To give her some privacy to get dressed, I get out of bed and busy myself in the living room folding the blanket from my makeshift bed on the couch. When she emerges, she's wearing jeans and a brown,

V-neck Henley almost the same color as her honey eyes. Her hair is braided neatly down the back of her head, and her bare cheeks are pink, freshly scrubbed.

"My turn." I give her a quick kiss on the lips as I pass her on my way to the bathroom.

I wash as best I can and put on clean jeans and a red plaid flannel shirt. My hair's hopeless, as always, so I fit my Braves hat snugly on my head, facing backward.

Back in the living room, Ramona tilts her head at me and smiles. "That's the hat I got you for graduation, isn't it?"

My face warms. I didn't think she remembered. "Yeah."

"You kept it all this time?" She stands in front of me and reaches up to turn the hat around on my head.

"Well, yeah. Why wouldn't I?" I grin. "We've already established I was crazy about you."

I still am, actually.

"Let's head over to the barn and see what Davie hasn't gotten to, yet," I suggest. "Then we can find some coffee."

"And breakfast."

"And breakfast. Don't worry, baby. I'll feed you."

***

"Well, hello, sleepy heads!" Jonah calls as we walk into the barn. Both he and Dan are here, along with Davie and my dad.

"I didn't know we were late to a barn party. What are y'all doin'?"

"Me and Uncle Kent are letting the city boys play cowboy," Davie says. "And getting some free labor to boot. Since you were sleeping in." He makes air quotes with his fingers around the last two words.

Ramona's cheeks turn red, and she dips her chin toward the barn floor. I feel my jaw tighten, and I ball my fists to keep them at my side. I'm not about to let my cousin embarrass Ramona.

"Get your mind out of the gutter," I growl at my cousin.

Dad heads off an argument by telling us about the farm tasks they've been teaching Dan and Jonah. After a few minutes, I'm laughing along with the guys instead of seething and glaring at Davie.

"They're doing pretty well too," he says. "A few more lessons, and they'll put you out of a job, Kevin."

Dan grins like a little kid. "Did you hear him, Ra? Tell Beth you heard it too, so she'll believe me."

Ramona laughs and shakes her head. "I'll make sure Beth knows what a competent cowboy you are."

"Anyway," my dad says, "we've got things handled here. Your mother made pancakes for breakfast at the house if you're hungry."

I look at Ramona, and she nods eagerly, so we head toward the house.

When we're almost there, Ramona stops. "Wait."

"What?"

"I don't hear the generator. Did your parents stop using it? How'd your mom make pancakes?"

I run my hands through my hair. I guess this is my opening to broach the topic I've been avoiding since she got here.

"We're only running it sometimes to save fuel," I start. "We're out of cold food now anyway, so we don't need the refrigerator running. We're turning the generator on to cook breakfast and dinner, and that's it. Besides..."

I pause long enough that she prompts me, a furrow between her brows. "Besides what?"

I sigh. "My parents and Aunt Cassie are leaving later today to drive to Charlotte to stay with my sister and her family for a while. It's been hard on them not to have running water and such."

"Yeah, I can imagine."

"My dad had a heart attack a while back, and he's still not totally better. My mom convinced him to go to Charlotte for her; really, it's to make sure he's okay. I'm worried about him overdoing it here. I'm going to move the generator over to my cabin so I can cook for me and Davie more easily."

She gives me a curious look. "That all makes sense. By the expression on your face, though, I feel like there's something you're not telling me."

I take a deep breath and tell her, "Until the utilities are back on, it's only me and Davie taking care of the farm. It means I have no backup help, and I can't leave. I know it's my turn to come visit you in Atlanta, but I ... I don't see how I can, at least for a while."

I feel awful; like I'm not holding up my side of this long-distance relationship. Like I've let her down after only two weeks as her boyfriend. Not a great start.

"Oh." She looks away, but not before I see her lips pressed together in a grimace. "That's understandable, right? You've got a lot going on here. I can't expect you to drop everything for me."

I shake my head. "You can and should expect me to drop everything for you. And you can tell me you're disappointed. I'm disappointed. And really sorry. I'd be with you every second of the day if I could."

I drop her hand to wrap her in a hug. When I let her go, she tilts her head, her watery eyes meeting mine.

"I *am* disappointed," she says. "Especially because I don't know when I can come back here again after this weekend. There's a project for work that's gearing up, and Katie needs all kinds of help with her wedding prep. It'll be hard for me to get away, too."

My ribs feel like they're tightening around my lungs as I try to pull in a deep breath of air. "I know. I'm sorry. This is hard."

"Yeah," she says quietly, dropping her eyes. She looks again sharply. "You can still come for Katie's wedding, though, right?"

"Yes. Absolutely. I'll be there."

I don't know yet what our situation will be by the end of December. I'll make sure I can be in Atlanta for New Year's Eve, even if it means hiring a worker or two to help Davie while I'm gone.

"So that's..." Ramona calculates in her head and groans, "more than two months until I see you again?"

A heavy weight settles onto my heart. "I guess so."

That's too long. Maybe I'll be able to leave the farm sooner after all. It depends on when Asheville's utilities come back on, and we start running more normally again. Atlanta's only three and a half hours away. It shouldn't be this hard.

"We'll figure it out," I tell her. "And in the meantime, we've still got pancakes waiting for us now, and hours together today before you leave."

Chapter Twelve

Ramona

♥

This can't be healthy. Seriously. If I thought I was dissatisfied with my life before my birthday, now I'm miserable. I wake up, and I think about Kevin. I drag myself to work, distracted by texts from and thoughts about Kevin. I somehow make it through the workday, completing the mindless tasks my team leader assigns me for the Super Bowl campaign. I'm disengaged, moving like a zombie through my day-to-day. The only bright spot, the only time I feel like myself, is during my nightly phone calls with Kevin.

Like I said, not normal. I've always been independent by nature. Dating is fun, but I've rarely felt like I needed a guy in my life to be happy. Now, my career feels stalled, my friends are busy with their own lives, and I haven't been this gaga over a man since ... well, since the last time Kevin and I were dating.

I hate that I haven't seen him in person for over a month. I hate that I won't see him in person for another whole month. I hate that things aren't stable enough in Asheville yet for Kevin's parents to go home. The electricity came back on a few days after the guys and I delivered the donated supplies. Internet services followed the electricity about a week later. Though water services came back around the same time as the Wi-Fi, the water coming out of the taps is yellow and unsafe to drink. The city immediately issued a boil water advisory. Kevin's thrilled to have indoor plumbing again, of course, but if the water isn't potable, he still has to manage and pay for weekly deliveries from a water tanker for the horses.

My heart squeezes thinking about the hardships they're facing in North Carolina. Kevin is such a good man: generous and hard working with a strong sense of loyalty and duty. Which is great, yet inconvenient now because it's his duties at the farm that are keeping him away from me.

He can't leave the farm right now, which I understand. At the same time, I miss him. Back in high school French class, I learned the French phrase for "I miss you" is *tu me manque*, which translates literally to *you are missing from me*. Kevin is missing from me, has been for almost ten years, though the ache is more acute now that we've reconnected.

"Guess what," Kevin prompts as soon as we connect on our video call that night. His hair is long and mussed—he hasn't stopped long enough to get a haircut since the flood almost two months ago. He looks good, though. The dark rings under his eyes show how hard all this has been for him, but his smile is easy, at least whenever he's talking to me.

I smile. "Ummm ... you saw a deer today."

He laughs. "Actually, yes, I did, but that's not my news."

"What's your news?"

His eyes sparkle. "The city lifted the boil water advisory."

I gasp. "The tap water is safe to drink again?"

"So they say. I've noticed it looks more and more clear these past few days. I'll wait until the end of the week before giving it to the horses, just in case. We still have some tanker water left to tide them over."

"That's a smart plan."

"I haven't told you the best part." His eyes are practically dancing now. In fact, his whole body is alight with motion—he's bouncing in his seat on the couch, hands fiddling with the drawstrings on his hoodie.

"What's the best part?"

"My parents are coming home Friday, which means I can ... what I mean is, I'd like to see if..." He blows out a breath. "Baby, can I come visit you this weekend?"

"Are you serious?" I squeal. "Yes, yes, yes, yes, yes, yes! Please come!" Tears flood my eyes, and I blink rapidly to keep them at bay.

"Are you sure? I know it's the weekend before Thanksgiving, so if you already have plans—"

I cut him off. "*You* are my plans. Kev, nothing would make me happier." Except him staying forever.

"Okay," he says with a wide grin. "I'll come. You don't have to beg."

I huff out a laugh, not bothering to stop the tears. Kevin stills on the screen and then shifts closer to the camera.

"Baby, are you crying?"

"Just a little," I blubber.

"I hope they're happy tears."

I bob my head. "They are." Tears of joy and relief and excitement. I'm feeling all the emotions knowing I'll be able to wrap my arms around Kevin in a few days.

"I'll bring you some fresh North Carolina apples," Kevin says. "The apple tree on the farm finally produced a few. Best apples you'll ever taste. I promise."

I laugh through the lump in my throat. "Sounds delicious. The apples will definitely be my favorite part of your visit."

***

After weeks when time felt like it dragged forward, the next few days are a whirlwind. I want everything to be perfect for Kevin's visit, so I plan meals, grocery shop, clean my apartment, and scour the internet for activities we can do together. Kevin's sister, Kristen, is driving their parents and Aunt Cassie from Charlotte back to the farm on Friday morning, giving Kevin the rest of the day Friday to spend time with them before leaving early Saturday morning to drive to my apartment in Atlanta. He'll head back home when I leave for work Monday morning. Two full days and nights together sound like heaven.

In a way, the long distance has been good for us. We've spent so much time talking—at least an hour each night before bed—that we know each other better now than ever before. We talk about the present: how our days went and projects we're working on. We also talk about the past: the last nine years we've been apart, and our childhoods, too. What I carefully avoid talking about is the future. He doesn't talk about it either, so maybe it's not something he thinks about or maybe, like me, he thinks about it obsessively and doesn't know how to bring it up without destroying what we have.

When Kevin calls Thursday night, I immediately launch into a monologue about the weekend and different activity options I've found.

"I found this food tour and cooking class combo where we would go to nine different places to try Atlanta food staples and learn to make biscuits. Doesn't that sound amazing?"

"Ramona."

I barely register Kevin saying my name as I plow forward.

"Or we can go to the Atlanta Botanical Garden. They have an incredible setup of holiday lights right now. Like millions of lights. It's so pretty—"

"Ramona."

This time, his voice is stronger, more insistent, so I pause. The serious tone catches me first, and I realize he's saying my name instead of calling me "baby" like he always does, and I know I'm not going to like what he has to say.

"I ... can't come. I'm so sorry, baby. I promise I'll make it up to you..."

Kevin is still talking; I don't hear him. It's like my head has filled up with white noise and the whooshing sound drowns out everything else. My throat constricts, and I swallow hard so I can breathe again. Of course he's not coming. In my rational brain, I know there must be a good reason, something he's explaining right now, probably. My emotional brain has already slipped into the driver's seat. *I'm not important to him. Trying to maintain this relationship long distance is hopeless. There's no place for me in his life.*

"Baby, please say something." The anguish in his voice brings my focus back to him.

I know I need to respond, listen to his explanation, try to pretend like he's not breaking my heart right now.

"You're not coming," I say slowly.

"No."

"Because..." I trail off, hoping he'll fill in the gaps of what he's probably already told me.

"Because of the snow. It's supposed to snow here overnight, and the roads will be icy. My sister doesn't want to drive back in those conditions. And the weather will create extra work here, too. I can't leave Davie to take care of it all on his own."

Again, my rational brain hears and understands the reasoning. This is beyond his control. He sounds truly pained and as upset as I am. My emotional brain slams on the brakes. I need to get off this phone call right now before I embarrass myself by crying again. This time, *not* happy tears.

"Okay," I say numbly.

"It's not okay. I'm not okay with this at all. I'm so sorry—"

"I just ... have to go."

I hang up and collapse onto the couch, my legs suddenly too heavy to hold me. I curl into myself as I hear my phone start ringing. I tune it out, listening to the dull thump of my heart in my chest.

I can't believe I did this again. I gave Kevin the power to crush me, and even if that wasn't his intention—now or nine years ago—it's exactly what has happened.

Kevin calls every thirty minutes until it's past eleven o'clock. I can't talk to him. Maybe it's immature to ignore his calls, but I'm emotionally flooded and can't. It's not only the canceled trip; it's the shock of reconnecting with Kevin, the trauma of the flooding in Asheville, the guilt of still having my normal life when so much has been devastated, the frustration with my job and career path, the heartache of wanting to be with Kevin and not seeing him enough. The highs and lows of the last two months have stretched me too thin, it's finally all catching up to me.

I call out of work Friday morning. Mostly I lie in bed zoning out and crying. Kevin tries calling a few more times; I still don't feel like I can talk to him. All day, the weather outside matches my mood. The weather system that brought snow to North Carolina drops rain here in Atlanta. Buckets of it falling from gray skies without a hint of sun peeking through.

By late afternoon, I feel stupid for letting the romance of seeing Kevin again in Asheville sweep me away. This isn't me. I'm practical and self-sufficient. Not someone who wastes an entire day in bed. And not someone who wastes nearly two months on a relationship with no future.

We have to break up. It's too hard. Better to cut my losses now than hang on, falling in love, only to end things a year from now. And I need to do it soon. Now. I pick up my phone to finally return Kevin's calls when I hear knocking on my front door.

I clutch my phone tighter, intending to ignore whoever's at the door. I'm in my pajamas, face blotchy and swollen from crying. I'm not expecting anyone.

The knocking becomes more insistent, enough that I leave the sanctuary of my bed and plod out to the living room. I'm definitely not answering the door now; in fact, I'm a little scared.

Then a muffled, recognizable voice calls from the other side of the door. "Baby?"

I'm dizzy for a moment—when did I last eat? I charge forward in a shock of adrenaline and fling open the front door.

Kevin fills my doorway, his long hair stringy and dripping from the rain, his eyes red. Before my mind understands what my body is doing, I jump into his arms, sobbing into his neck.

He's here.

Chapter Thirteen

Kevin

♥

I catch Ramona when she jumps, but barely. After stabilizing her body against mine, I cinch my arms around her back and walk carefully forward into the apartment. When we pass the threshold, I kick the door closed behind us. Finding the couch, I drop into the corner, rearranging Ramona so she's snug in my lap.

I take a moment to catch my breath. After waiting for the snow to stop falling this morning and then making sure the horses were taken care of, I told Davie I'd be back tomorrow and hopped in the car. I raced here, probably none too safely. I had to see her, touch her.

In the turmoil of the last twenty-four hours, having her on my lap and being able to hold her in my arms feels like a sweet relief. Our time away from each other has been torture. The only thing that helped me through—other than taking care of my horses—was talking to her on the phone at night. At least I could hear her voice, see her face, if I couldn't hold and kiss her.

It gutted me to have to call and disappoint her. Again. Seems like that's what I'm best at as Ramona's boyfriend. And she hung up so abruptly and didn't answer when I called back over and over. When she shut me out, I lost it. I had to know what she was feeling and thinking. I had to know she could forgive me. *Please* let her forgive me.

I've never needed any woman like I need Ramona.

I look at her in my arms. Her face is still nestled in the crook of my neck, and I can't tell if my shirt is wet from the rain or her tears. Squeezing her tighter, I place a gentle kiss on her head. She lifts her face to mine, and I note the puffiness around her eyes, the tear streaks along her cheeks.

My stomach lurches knowing it's my fault she's been crying. I lean forward and kiss away a tear sitting on the apple of her cheek. I kiss away a tear rolling down her chin. I kiss tear after tear until there are none left, and she's staring at me, breathless and still. I kiss the corner of her mouth, testing her reaction.

She shifts her face, bringing her lips even with mine, just inches away. I want so badly to close the distance. This would be our first kiss in a month, and I'm not sure I have any right to it. Or if she wants me to.

Then, miracle of miracles, *she* leans forward and kisses *me*, softly and tentatively at first, then searching and desperate. I let her set the pace, answering her lips with my own in a fervent hunger to let her know how much she means to me.

Eventually, she angles back, and I study her face. She's no longer crying; her lips are pinched and her eyes dart to mine and away again.

"You're here."

I hold her tighter. "How could I be anywhere else?"

"I needed you," she accuses.

I rub small circles across her back. "And I'm here."

"But you couldn't come. I thought..."

"I have to leave in the morning." I wish I could stay for the weekend, like we'd planned. *I wish I could stay forever*, a voice in the back of my mind whispers, which surprises me. I've never seriously considered moving away from my farm before. I love that farm. It's my family's legacy and my responsibility. My assumption has been that eventually Ramona would have to move to North Carolina if we're going to be together. For the first time, I wonder if I'd be open to moving instead.

"You still came."

I look her in the eye. "I did."

"Why?"

"You wouldn't answer my calls."

She ducks her head. "I was mad at you. Or rather, I was hurt."

"I don't want you to be mad at me. I don't want to hurt you."

"I know." She says it softly, almost a whisper.

I place a finger under her chin and nudge her face up so she's looking me in the eyes. "It might still happen sometimes."

"I know," she says again, stronger this time.

"You have to talk to me, though. Please. We can work it out together."

She closes her eyes. "This is really hard, Kev."

It's *really* hard. I'm losing my mind being away from her all the time. "Yeah. What could make it easier?"

She doesn't hesitate. "Seeing you more often."

"I'd love to see you more often. Any ideas?"

Her forehead wrinkles as she considers. I'm thinking, too. "My parents will be back home soon, for one. That'll make it easier for me to get away from the farm."

"I'll be busy with the Super Bowl ad at work for the next couple of months, and Katie's wedding too over the next month. Katie will mostly need me on Saturdays, and I could work more during the week to make time for weekend visits. What if we meet halfway sometimes?"

I shift Ramona to one side as I reach for my pocket and pull out my phone. To my disappointment, she slips off my lap and onto her own couch cushion, but she stays close to my side.

I type into my maps app, and we look at the results together.

"Halfway ... let's see." I squint into my phone. "Looks like some-where around the Georgia-North Carolina border?"

She cranes her head to see the screen. "What's there?"

I zoom in on the map. "Mostly forest, it looks like. Uh, a state park, a wildlife management area."

She frowns. "That doesn't sound promising."

"Ah, wait! Look. Dillard, Georgia." I google the town and start reading aloud from the website. "Experience Dillard, Georgia ... gateway to the Great Smoky Mountains ... adventure abounds ... outdoor adventures, natural attractions, antiques, art and museums, dining, shopping."

For the first time since I arrived, Ramona sits tall, her shoulders set back with an air of hopefulness. She smiles, and it's so beautiful I can feel my heart expand in my chest.

"That sounds great! How about this? Once a month, we'll do a full weekend visit, alternating who drives to who. And once a month, we'll meet in Dillard, Georgia, or somewhere nearby, on a Sunday and spend the day there together."

"Perfect." Well, not *quite* perfect. Perfect would be seeing her every second of every day. Given the circumstances, though, seeing her every couple of weeks sounds much better than what we're doing now.

We plan to meet in Dillard, Georgia a couple of weeks from now, and I put away my phone.

Ramona snuggles into my arm. "You have to leave in the morning?"

I sigh. "Yeah."

"So, what do you want to do now? We could stay in. I haven't eaten since ... well I'm not sure when, so we could go get some food or something."

I eye her outfit—baggy, plaid pajama pants and an oversized t-shirt. Her hair's up in a loose bun, with strands falling onto her face.

I grin and tug on the bottom hem of her shirt. "Stay in, I think."

She looks down at herself and blushes. "Oh, yeah."

I snap my fingers and stand. "Hold that thought. I have something in my truck that might help your hunger."

I start to walk toward the door but she clings to my arm, so I stoop and kiss her forehead.

"Baby, I'll be right back. And then I swear I won't leave your side until tomorrow morning."

Chapter Fourteen

Ramona

♥

True to his word, Kevin's back inside within five minutes. He's holding a paper grocery sack.

"I promised you apples," he says.

I laugh. "You still brought the apples?"

He shrugs. "Of course."

He reaches into the bag and pulls out an apple. He hands it to me, and, without ceremony, I take a big bite. It tastes like pure apple cider, juicy and crisp. I close my eyes.

I want to make Kevin smile, and this apple is ridiculously good, so I say, "Oh my gosh, this is the best apple I've ever had. Seriously, it's like what you imagine an apple should taste like. A real apple's apple."

He grins and kisses my nose. "You're cute."

I like it when he thinks I'm cute. He chuckles and shakes his head, and he looks at me with such adoration in his eyes.

Less than an hour ago, I was going to call him to break up. Then he was at my door, looking sexy and being sweet, and now I want to soak him up as much as I can before he has to leave in the morning.

Plus, we have a plan now. We'll see each other every two weeks, which is better than going a month or more between in-person visits, though still not enough. It works for now; it works for the short term.

What happens in the long term with this long-distance relationship is the elephant in the room. We both know that when we finally talk about it, there's no going back; we'll run into the insurmountable problem of geography and have to end things.

So, let's not talk about it.

We need to eat more than apples for dinner, so after changing my clothes and washing my face, I pull out some of the groceries I bought in anticipation of Kevin's original visit. Together, we cook chicken tacos, though Kevin's not much of a chef. When I ask him to chop the bell peppers, he neglects to remove the core, and I have to pick the seeds out before adding the peppers to the pan.

"It's a good thing you're hot," I tease.

He leans back against the kitchen counter and folds his arms. His grin turns cocksure and devastating.

"You think I'm hot?"

I answer him with an ardent kiss. When I step away, he tries to pull me back. I shake my head and return to my spot at the stove.

"No," I say.

"No, what?"

I smirk at him over my shoulder. "No, I don't think you're hot."

His laugh is deep and rich, and I wish I could bottle the way it makes me feel warm inside.

"Yeah, I don't believe that for a second. It's fine though because I happen to think you're pretty hot, too." His arms encircle my waist from behind, and he rests his chin on the top of my head.

I swat him away with a spatula. "Stop distracting me. I don't want to burn dinner."

Still lingering behind me, he runs his fingers over my arms. "I'll eat it anyway."

His fingers feel warm on my skin; the sensation makes me shiver. "That's sweet, but this is the first time I've cooked for you, and I want you to be impressed."

"I'm already impressed with you," he murmurs in my ear.

My breath hitches, and I step back from the stove, spinning around to face him.

"Kev," I say as I cup his cheeks in my hands. "Focus."

He takes a breath and lets it out slowly. "Okay. I'm focused."

"I'm so happy you're here. The boundaries we talked about before I came to Asheville last month still apply. I don't want to give you the wrong idea. I'm not ready."

"Understood. No pressure, I promise." He frowns. "So, I'm on the couch tonight?"

I hesitate. "Well, if you can promise you'll behave—"

"I promise," he says quickly. "Really and seriously. I respect you and your boundaries."

***

The next morning, I don't like saying goodbye, but having a plan in place helps. It doesn't stop me from clinging to him or walking him out to his truck or kissing him against his truck for thirty minutes before I finally let him go.

As he pulls around the corner and out of sight, the countdown clock in my head starts ticking: fifteen days.

Chapter Fifteen

Kevin

♥

Not only do Ramona and I follow through on our plans to meet up in Dillard, Georgia, we talk to each other on the phone the entire drive there from our respective houses.

The trip is shorter for me—closer to an hour and a half than Ramona's two hours—so I park when I arrive and wait for her. We decided to begin our morning together at a living history museum representing life in Appalachia in the 1800s and 1900s. Well, Ramona decided. I don't care what we're doing if I get to see her. I could tell she had fun putting together the itinerary though, so I agreed to whatever plan she came up with.

When I finally see her silver coupe pull into the parking lot, I practically jump out of the truck. Her engine's barely off before she's out of the car and jumping into my arms. I chuckle to myself. I don't need to wonder if she's as into me as I'm into her.

I find her lips with mine and bask in the feel of her. It's been two weeks since I touched her, and at this moment, I don't understand how I was able to survive that long. Everything in me settles when Ramona's in my arms.

It's a chilly day, and she's wearing jeans with a soft, dark red sweater I can't seem to stop touching. Her cheeks are pink, whether from the cold air or the kissing, I'm not sure.

She studies me and fingers the hair on my neck.

"I know, I know. I promise I'll get a haircut before the wedding."

"Thank you," she says. "And no hat, please."

I grin. "What, you mean I shouldn't wear my ten-year-old ball cap to a formal wedding?"

"No."

"What if I wear a top hat?"

She laughs. "No top hat, either."

"That's no fun." I heave an exaggerated sigh. "Well, I guess it's jeans and boots, then."

The glare she shoots me is enough to make even the most hardened criminal sit up straight in church. I laugh and smack a kiss on her cheek.

"I'm kidding, baby. I know how to dress."

She raises her eyebrows. "Do you? Because this is the dressiest I've ever seen you."

She motions to my boot cut jeans—they're my best pair but still look worn in the knees—and flannel button-down shirt.

"Maybe you should send me a picture of your outfit ahead of the wedding," she suggests.

"No need. Just prepare to be dazzled."

***

After a lengthy and public parking lot hello, we walk into the museum hand-in-hand. I pay our admission fees, and we're free to roam around the log buildings of the outdoor village. On the porches of the cabins, demonstrators sit and show off skills from long ago like weaving, blacksmithing, even a banjo player. I'm disappointed to see they're not dressed in period costumes, though. Man, I love when these places do that, especially when the people pretend they have no idea what a phone or car is.

The historic village replica has a chapel—a log building on top of stacks of wide stone centered in a garden of trees. Several stained-glass windows designate the simple structure as special. Inside, the one room is dark and peaceful. Three rows of rustic, wooden benches against either wall form an aisle down the center leading to a simple pulpit. An exhibit is set up in the chapel about shape note music. I read the placard at the front of the chapel while Ramona moves around the room to better see the stained glass. When I finish reading, I swivel my head to find her. She's walking down the aisle toward me, a smile on her face.

Suddenly, I'm overwhelmed. The image of Ramona, walking down the aisle, makes it hard to breathe. I imagine her in a white gown, her hair up in some sort of fancy 'do, ready to marry me. My heart thrums and aches with the need for that vision to come true. I blink back tears as she reaches me.

She tilts her head, studying my face. "What's wrong?"

I clear my throat and wrap an arm around her waist to pull her into me. "Nothing at all."

We finish exploring the museum and head back to the parking lot, ready for our next destination. Ramona's plan is for us to have lunch at the famous Dillard House Restaurant, where they serve family-sized platters of authentic southern cooking.

It's only a nine-minute drive from the museum, so we each take our own car. A white wooden sign greets us as we drive into the parking lot, a beautiful mountain view behind it. I live in the mountains, yet a good mountain landscape can still stop me in my tracks. I'm not sure I'll ever be desensitized.

Similarly, I hope my heart never stops skipping a beat when I see Ramona's smile. She gives me that smile now, holding my hand as we walk up the pathway toward the restaurant.

I put my hand to my heart and shake my head. "Ramona," I whisper.

She makes a face. "I don't like when you call me Ramona."

I chuckle. "That's your name."

Her bottom lip turns out in an adorable pout. "Not to you."

I wrap my arms around her, pulling her close, nipping at that pouty lip. "What's your name to me then?"

"Baby," she says and my stomach swoops.

I back her up against the cobblestone wall on the side of the restaurant and put my lips against her ear. "You like when I call you baby?"

"Mmhmm," she whimpers.

I kiss a trail from the side of her neck to her throat, then back up, where I capture her earlobe between my teeth. She gasps and grips the front of my jacket with both hands.

"Let's go make out in the truck," I murmur into her ear.

"I thought we were going to have lunch." Her voice is breathy and hot.

"I'm not hungry." For food, at least.

She laughs and pushes gently against my chest. "Well, I am!"

I groan, stepping back. "Are you sure?" She gives me a scolding look, so I hold up my hands in surrender. "Fine, let's eat lunch."

As much as I would have loved skipping food for more time with my lips against Ramona's skin, I can't say I'm disappointed in the restaurant. The food is delicious, with huge portions that leave me stuffed.

From here, we leave our cars and walk to the Dillard Boardwalk for shopping. We find a cool old-timey general store, antique shops, and a Merry Christmas Shop. We buy old-fashioned candy, jars of jam, and Christmas presents for our friends and family. Neither of us are particularly into antiquing, but as we wander the hodgepodge of vintage items, we create detailed histories of the lives of fictional previous owners.

A tall side table with a clock face imprinted under the glass top was originally the property of a Mrs. Temps, who would invite unwitting passers-by for tea. When seated at the table with Mrs. Temps, time stood still so when someone emerged from a twenty-minute visit with her, they stumbled outside to find twenty years had passed.

A large, framed painting of a river with trees on each bank was done by a man who dreamed of being an artist. Instead, his father forced him to take over the family business running a mortuary in a small, mountain town. The man hung the painting on the wall of his office at the funeral home and imagined rafting away on the river to his freedom.

Admittedly, these stories are all Ramona. Unbelievable that this woman can make an antique store fun. She's a natural storyteller, which I know is one of the reasons she likes the idea of telling a company's story through marketing. If only she could do that in her current job. She doesn't talk about it much, but I can tell she's unhappy there. She never wants to spend much time telling me about her projects or colleagues at work, while I go into too much detail about my horses and how I'm managing the farm. Instead, she talks almost wistfully about what she'd like to be doing—helping small, locally-owned companies, maybe nonprofits, get the word out about who they are, their products and services.

I wish she would talk things through with me more. Pushing her into a conversation about finding a new job would veer dangerously into the topic we've silently agreed not to discuss: the future. I would love Ramona to move to Asheville, but I don't know if that's something she's willing to do. Certainly not right now, when jobs are scarce enough for the people who've lived there their whole lives. And housing remains a challenge too, and likely will for a long time. Of course, she could marry me and move into the cottage to solve that one...

I shake my head to dislodge the thought. She walked back into my life literally a few months ago, and I'm already seriously thinking about marriage; twice now today. That's where I'm at. This is what she does to me. What she's always done to me.

Before long, we learn most everything in Dillard closes at five o'clock. We walk back to the cars and, separately, we drive two miles up the road to a farm-to-table restaurant on an actual farm.

Neither of us are terribly hungry since we ate so much at lunch. We split an appetizer and a dessert. Both are delicious.

"I tell you what," I joke, "I may need to start jogging or something if we're going to eat like this once a month."

Ramona's lips pinch at my words, and she doesn't respond.

"What's wrong?"

She sighs. "It's just ... today has been so incredible."

I chuckle. "It has. Isn't that a good thing?"

"Not when it's almost over, and it'll be three long weeks before I see you again."

I reach across the table and take her hand. "True. Just think, though, the next time you see me, we'll be together for a whole week. Hanging out through the post-Christmas slump. Getting dressed up and fancy for Katie's wedding. Dancing and kissing into the new year."

Her smile is back. "That sounds amazing."

I catch her eyes and hold them. "Everything with you is amazing."

Her cheeks turn the cutest shade of pink, so I flash her a grin.

"You ready to head out?" I ask, pulling out my wallet to pay the bill.

Now it's her turn to grin, her eyes shining. "Didn't you mention something earlier about making out in your truck?"

My hand freezes with my fingers around the credit card midway to setting it on the table. Did she say what I think she said? I lick my lips before snapping the card on the table with a flourish.

"Yes, ma'am," I manage to croak out. I clear my throat. "We could ... uh, we could do that."

Her grin shifts to a smirk. "You're not in a rush to get home?"

I wink. "Baby, for you, I've got nothin' but time."

Chapter Sixteen

Ramona

♥

One week since I saw Kevin in Dillard; two weeks until Katie and Jonah's wedding. Katie called all hands on deck to help her assemble centerpieces, but Beth's got a sick kid, and Jonah's across town helping his parents with a car issue. Katie's parents don't fly in from Wisconsin until Christmas Eve.

So, it ends up being the two of us filling large cylindrical glass vases with gold and white ball ornaments of various sizes and textures. The result is simple and elegant, which is exactly the vibe Katie's going for.

"These are beautiful," I tell Katie. "Your wedding is going to be amazing."

She beams. "Thank you! I'm slowly chipping away at the to-do list. And Jonah's a big help, as, of course, are you and Beth."

I feign a sitting-down curtsy. "At your service."

"Between your big project at work, and helping with my wedding prep, and trying to see your long-distance boyfriend, I'm surprised you have time to sleep."

"Who says I do?" I quip.

Katie grins before her face turns serious. "How are things going with you and Kevin?"

I hesitate. "I know you're not his biggest fan—"

Katie shakes her head. "I don't dislike Kevin. I hate his mountains. And I didn't love the way you fell apart back in college when you guys broke up or whatever. If you say it's all water under the bridge, I'm fine."

I wave my hand in front of my face. "That was all so long ago. No one's fault. Neither of us knew how the other felt."

"So how are things now?"

"Yeah, um ... good. You know?" I pause. "It's just whenever I'm with him, it's like this all-consuming *thing*. Like nothing else exists, nothing else matters. And then when we're apart, I feel so ... blah. Like I'm only myself anymore when we're together. The rest of my life feels so dull, so purposeless."

"That started months before we went to Asheville, though."

I shrug. "Maybe."

"You two always had this intense connection, which isn't a bad thing. But, Ra, if you weren't happy in your life without Kevin, a relationship with him isn't going to magically make you happy. So, taking Kevin out of the equation, are you happy with your life?"

I slowly shake my head. I don't have to think about it. It's like that one movement breaks open a vial of truth serum in my brain, and I pour it all out to my best friend.

"What aren't you happy with?"

"My job."

"What about your job?"

"I don't want to sell luxuries to millionaires. I want to help people; make a difference in the world. All we experienced and saw and heard about in Asheville only made me want that more."

"Okay, so what are you going to do?"

I hang my head. "I don't know. What can I do? Start looking for a new job? And then it gets complicated again with Kevin. If I'm looking for a new job anyway, do I look for one in North Carolina? Here in Atlanta? It feels like too much too soon."

Katie stops arranging the ornaments in her vase and looks me straight in the eye. "Do you love him?"

I slowly nod my head. Again, I don't have to think about it. "Yeah. I do."

"Then you should have a conversation with him like an adult."

I groan. "It's too soon, right? We've been dating less than three months, and I can count on one hand—one hand!—the number of days we've spent together in person during that time."

"I can't make that decision for you. All I can say is if you're making changes in your life, you need to decide whether and how Kevin fits into them. Maybe it means you two do the long-distance thing a while longer."

I cringe. I swear I hate the phrase "long distance" more each time I hear it. I'm starting to realize I need either no distance at all from Kevin or complete and total distance. I'm not sure the first is possible, and I can't stand the thought of the second.

Chapter Seventeen

Kevin

♥

On the Friday after Christmas, I drive down to Atlanta. My family knows not to expect me back until the new year, and my dad and Davie are in charge at the farm in the meantime. It's been so long since I've left the farm for more than a single day or night, and I'm surprised at the lightness I feel—the sense of freedom. Mostly it's because I'm driving toward Ramona, but also that I'm escaping. I love the farm. I love Asheville. I never want to live anywhere else. But the past few months have been *hard*.

Once the Biltmore opened back up, other tourist destinations downtown and in West Asheville followed suit. Biltmore Village and the River Arts District businesses haven't been as fortunate. For residents, housing and work are hard to find with the devastation to homes and businesses in the area.

In addition to running the farm, I go out and do what I can to help, volunteering through my church and a couple other community organizations. Though me and my family were largely spared, my community is hurting. It's a heavy mental and emotional load. I'm looking forward to leaving all those worries behind for a while as I celebrate the holidays with my girlfriend in Atlanta.

I start grinning as I round the corner into her neighborhood. In some ways, long distance has been good for us. It's given us the opportunity to talk a lot and catch up on the last nine years. In other ways, it's been torture. I'm a physical touch kind of guy and talking on the phone, even a video call, isn't the same as being able to touch her. And I'm not even talking about touching her in a sensual way, just holding her hand, kissing the top of her head, and wrapping her in my arms will all be highlights of this next week.

It starts as soon as Ramona opens her apartment door and throws herself into my embrace. I inhale the familiar fruity scent of her hair as I run my palm down her back. She's dressed for a cozy evening at home in yoga pants and a hoodie, fluffy socks on her feet.

"Baby, you didn't have to get all dressed up for me," I tease.

She blushes. Honestly, I love that she feels comfortable enough to be herself with me. Dressed up, dressed down, doesn't matter to me.

She tilts her head at me. "You got a haircut."

"I told you I would."

I went this morning to the same old barber who's been cutting my hair since I was a kid, minus the years I was away at college. He gave me an undercut, which is *not* the same as I normally get. I ended up liking how my hair looked when I unintentionally let it grow out, so I wanted to keep some of that. My new cut is shorter on the sides and back, with some length on top still. Today it's messy. I didn't style it, though I should have since it's the first time Ramona's seeing it. I brought styling cream to make it fancier for the wedding.

Ramona's still studying me. "I like it," she finally says. "You look sexy."

My heart speeds up, and I smirk. "So, like always?"

She raises her eyebrows and pulls on my arm until I'm inside her apartment.

"We're having a movie marathon."

"Yeah?"

She gestures toward the couch, where the coffee table is loaded with bowls of chips and packages of cookies. "All classic movies. I bought lots of snacks."

Cuddled up on the couch with Ramona all afternoon? "Sounds perfect."

"Go put your suitcase away in my room, and then I have a surprise for you."

I grin. "I love surprises."

I do as I'm told and carry my suitcase to Ramona's bedroom. I'm guessing, like the last time I spent the night, she'll be okay with spooning in bed, but nothing else. And I totally respect that. My gut tells me that, though Ramona obviously loves talking and touching and spending time with me, she's not all in yet. Which is fine. She's being cautious, and while part of me envies that, another part of me knows it's not in my nature to hold back my heart. I'll stick around and show her how I feel until she's certain I'm not going anywhere. I don't want her to do anything she's not comfortable with.

Back in the living room, Ramona stands by the couch, hands behind her back.

"Are you ready?" she asks, eyes twinkling.

"I'm ready."

She pulls her arms out in front of her, showcasing a large pair of fuzzy, red and white striped socks with green patches on the heels and toes. Those are for her, right? No way in hell I'll be wearing the fluffy monstrosities.

"I got you cozy Christmas socks!"

Her enthusiasm is adorable. Maybe I could wear the socks. I chuckle. "I see that. And I'm guessing you want me to wear them for the movie marathon?"

"Of course!" She must see the resignation on my face, because she teases, "You're lucky because I almost got you the ones with reindeer on the toes and big, fluffy white trim around the ankles. I can still switch them out if you'd like." Her eyes twinkle mischievously.

I grab the socks from her hand. "I love these! They're amazing! Best cozy Christmas socks I've ever seen! My new favorite piece of clothing!"

She laughs. "Okay, okay."

I lift my eyebrows. "Too much?"

Pinching her pointer finger and thumb together, she says, "Just a smidge."

We settle onto the couch, and I put on my new socks. I hate to admit it; they're *very* comfortable. They look ridiculous, especially on a grown man, but my feet do feel cozier.

Ramona starts us out with Christmas movies—*It's a Wonderful Life*, the original *Miracle on 34th Street* with Natalie Wood, *White Christmas*—punctuated with the promised snacks and delivery Chinese food.

As *White Christmas* winds down with snow finally falling on General Waverly's Vermont inn, I check the time on my phone. It's ten at night already, and I was up, as usual, at six this morning to make sure everything was set at the farm for my absence. I wouldn't mind going to bed now. Ramona has other plans.

"Now for the main event."

I can't help my smile, even as I'm stifling a yawn. "What's the main event?"

She holds her hand to her chest as if she can't believe I'd ask such a question. "Well, *Casablanca* of course! We have to watch *Casablanca*."

I pull her closer, so her back is against my chest and her head rests on my shoulder. "We absolutely do."

I fall asleep before the end of the movie. When I wake, the TV is dark, and Ramona is sleeping in my arms. I'd be happy to stay like this the rest of the night except the position I'm in makes my back ache, and my bladder is about to burst. Slowly, so I don't wake her, I stand with Ramona in my arms. She stirs before resting her head on my shoulder. I carry her to her room and put her on the bed. After I get her settled under the covers, I duck into the bathroom.

When I come back, I slip into bed on the other side. When I roll over to face Ramona, her eyes are open.

"I thought maybe you went to sleep on the couch," she whispers.

I freeze. "Do you want me to?"

"No." She runs her hand over my cheek. "Stay here with me."

"Always," I promise.

***

Over the next few days, we see everything in Atlanta. Okay, not really, but my girl loves making itineraries. We do a food tour that includes a biscuit making class at the end, where I apparently "overworked" the dough and made my biscuits too tough. I eat them anyway.

We also visit the Atlanta Botanical Garden one night to see their famous light display. There's one boardwalk that's surrounded by trees with curtains of lights hanging down that dance in sync to Christmas music. It's amazing. They do not oversell this thing.

We take a day and go to historical and cultural sites like the King Center, the Jimmy Carter Library, and the Atlanta History Center. Some I'd been to before, back when I was in college—I was a history minor, and the city made for a great classroom—some are new for both of us.

Then, we shift into wedding mode. Katie and Jonah's wedding, I mean, not ours. Although I still don't hate the idea.

There's a joint wedding party celebration where I get to know Dan and Jonah better. I ignored them rudely when they came up to the farm a few months ago. Now, coming off several days and nights in a row with Ramona, I'm more willing to leave her side tonight.

They're fun guys, ones I'd be friends with even if they weren't the husbands, or soon to be, of my girlfriend's best friends.

I figure they're Braves fans if they like baseball, living in Atlanta and all. I'm not sure they know I am, too. So, when Dan mentions the young pitcher Anthopoulos recently signed, I jump in.

"It gives them a better shot at the pennant this season, for sure."

The guys assess me. "You a Braves fan?" Jonah asks.

"My whole life."

Dan crosses his arms and narrows his eyes. "Who was your favorite player growing up?"

I shift on my feet. "Well, this is going to sound weird, but I loved Martin Prado."

Jonah laughs. "Really? Not Chipper? Or even Maddux or Andruw Jones?"

I shrug. "I met him once at an autograph signing. He was nice."

Dan bobs his head. "That's cool, man."

Jonah slaps me on the back. "Yeah, I'll allow it."

A bout of loud laughter from across the room pulls my attention away from the conversation. Ramona throws her head back as she laughs, her hand on Beth's shoulder. The movement tosses her hair, some strands glinting an almost gold color in the overhead lights. She looks beautiful.

When I turn back to Dan and Jonah, they stare at me.

"You really like her, huh?" Dan asks.

I rub my chin. "Yeah."

I more than *like* Ramona. I'm not telling these guys before I tell her, though.

Dan and Jonah exchange a look, and Jonah leans toward me, holding eye contact. "Okay."

"Okay?" I ask.

Dan dips his head. "Yeah, okay. Just don't hurt her."

"I promise."

***

My time with Ramona, which seemed luxuriously long when it started, passes unbelievably fast. New Year's Eve has arrived already—Katie and Jonah's wedding day. I wait in the living room for Ramona to be ready to go, pacing circles around the couch. Ramona needs to be at the venue early to get dressed and ready with the wedding party. I'll tag along and hang out until it's time for the ceremony to start.

Of course, I'm dressed already. She hasn't seen my suit yet, and I'm questioning it now. I don't own a suit. Or at least, I didn't. Yes, I'm a thirty-one-year-old man who doesn't own a suit. There's not much call for formal wear on the farm. When I go to church, I wear khaki pants with a collared shirt. I over-promised when we were in Dillard, and I'll be damned if I embarrass Ramona in front of all her friends.

So, I went shopping. More specifically, I went to a small business in downtown Asheville specializing in tailored suits. It was *not* cheap. I have to admit I have never had clothing fit me like this before. I went with classic dark gray, single breasted. I liked the idea of the vest thing, so I got a three-piece. I bought a burgundy tie to go with it. I know Ramona's wearing gold, and since she's a bridesmaid, I can't match her unless I want to look like I'm supposed to be a groomsman.

Anyway, now I'm worried I went overboard. Is it possible to be dressed *too* fancy for a New Year's Eve wedding?

My fears fly out the window as soon as Ramona sees me. She stops short, her eyes raking up my body. She puffs out a breath, as if she's been holding it in. When her gaze gets to my face, her eyes are glassy. Lips parted, she steps closer to me, erasing the distance. With her freshly washed face, the flush on her cheeks and neck are obvious as she runs her hands up and down my coat sleeves.

My chest inflates as I reach up and fiddle with my tie. Listen, I know I'm a decently handsome guy, yet I've never felt as attractive as I do right now, and let me tell you, it's a turn on. I can literally feel how much Ramona wants me through the heat of her hands.

I smirk as I peer into her face. "Hey, what's up baby?"

"Kev ... you look ... this suit..." Her cheeks turn redder as she trails off.

My smile widens. "This old thing? Do you like it?"

She licks her lips. "Yeah. Like a lot." She stands on her tiptoes and brushes a kiss against my lips. "A little too much if I want to be on time."

I slide one hand onto the small of her back and rest the other on the back of her neck. "Eh. We've got a few minutes. And you're not wearing makeup yet."

"So?" She steps closer, her feet tucked between mine.

"So, there's nothing for me to mess up." I flash a wicked grin as I lower my lips to hers.

We're only twenty minutes late to meet the bride.

Chapter Eighteen

Once the hairstylist and makeup artist have primped and prodded us within an inch of our lives, Beth helps me put my dress on. Next, I help with hers, and we both help the bride.

Katie looks gorgeous. Her white gown is form-fitted, with long sleeves. The lace, with a beige lining underneath, covers her chest all the way up to her neck. Her back is exposed to her natural waist. She wears her auburn-red hair loose around her face in waves.

"Oh my gosh." Beth flaps a hand in front of her eyes. "I want to cry, but I know I can't, or I'll ruin my makeup. You look so beautiful."

I blink back my own tears. "You really do."

Katie beams. "Thank you. I'm so happy. And so glad I get to share this with both of you."

"Aww, come here you guys!" Beth pulls us both in for a hug.

When we step back, she looks at me knowingly. "This will be you before long."

Katie winks at me and smirks while I try to swallow past the panic rising in my throat. I paste a smile on my lips and change the subject.

"How much longer do we have?"

Beth checks her watch. "Still about thirty minutes."

I clap my hands. "We need shoes!"

Beth pulls her shoes out of her bag and looks around. "Where are yours, Ra?"

"Oh, um…" I dart my eyes around the room before I remember. "Shoot. I left them in the car. Let me text Kevin to get them for me. He has my keys anyway."

About ten minutes later, a knock sounds on the door of the dressing room. I swing it open, and Katie calls out, "Don't let him see me! It will ruin the big reveal!"

"Okay, okay!" I answer, stepping into the hallway and pulling the door closed behind me.

I turn to face Kevin, and he's staring at me, mouth open, holding a shoebox.

"Hey. Thanks." I reach my hand out to take the box from him. He doesn't move.

I tilt my head. "Are you okay, Kev?"

He runs his hand over his chin and clears his throat. "Wow. I mean … you look incredible, baby."

I *am* partial to this dress. Katie is not a proponent of the whole "ugly bridesmaid dress" trope. Being that this is a New Year's Eve wedding, she chose gold sequin dresses for Beth and me. The dress is floor-length, the skirt sleek, with room to move. It has a ruched waist and cap sleeves, with a V neckline that dips low enough to show some cleavage, while maintaining a classy look. The hair stylist gave Beth and me the same loose waves as Katie, though my hair isn't nearly as long as hers.

The warmth in Kevin's eyes heats me from the inside out. I may be dressed up tonight, but it's the same look he gives me when I'm in sweats, or jeans, or when I'm crying into his chest in the middle of the night. It's a look of awe and adoration. Love.

Of course, Kevin looks super hot tonight, too. The suit he's wearing accentuates all his best features; it's tighter around his thighs and upper arms, tapered in at the waist. His blue eyes pop against the deep red of his tie. He has his hair slicked back in a style that begs me to sink my fingers in and muss it up. Instead, I run my palms against the lapels of his jacket.

"We make a pretty good couple, don't we?" I tease.

"The best." His tone is serious, his eyes soft. He leans in close and murmurs against my ear, "How mad would Katie get if I messed up your makeup?"

My heart speeds up. I push him away, laughing. "Not happening." I run the tips of my fingers along his jawline and smirk. "At least not before the wedding starts."

***

The ceremony is beautiful. As the pastor talks about everlasting love and the hard work of commitment, sharing joys and challenges throughout a lifetime, my eyes keep wandering to Kevin in the congregation. Every time, he's already looking at me with an intensity in his eyes that thrills and scares me. Journeying through life together—can I give him that? I want to so badly. Can *he* give *me* that?

I find Kevin after the ceremony—we already did wedding party photos beforehand, so now the photographer is getting some of the bride and groom. We walk into the reception together, Kevin's hand guiding me on the small of my back.

I'm immediately in awe. I know about most of the decorations, of course. I helped arrange them. Seeing the room pulled together like this is breathtaking. The color scheme is gold against black, with lighting perfectly situated around the room to make the gold shine and sparkle. The cake is five tiers of gleaming gold.

It's already been a long day when the dancing starts. Kevin pulls me to my feet. How can I say no to his eager grin? With all we've experienced, both back in college and since we reunited in September, we've never danced together. We move across the floor almost as one, so smoothly and ridiculously in sync. I anticipate his every move, and he follows through, guiding me around the floor with the smallest nudges. He's glorious. We're glorious together.

Around eleven, Katie and Jonah cut the cake. Kevin and I decide we need a break from dancing anyway, so we each grab a slice and return to our table for the first time in hours. Kevin picks up two flutes of champagne on the way. I settle into my chair while Kevin pulls his closer, sweeping my legs onto his lap.

My slice of cake is a decadent chocolate, while Kevin's looks like something with raspberries. I take a bite of mine and let it melt in my mouth, closing my eyes. I open them and scoop up another bite, holding it out toward Kevin.

"You have to try this." I lean closer, lifting my fork to his mouth before meeting his gaze. His eyes are dark, the intensity I saw during the ceremony back in full force. Shifting his head forward, Kevin closes his lips around the fork and pulls back slowly, never breaking eye contact.

My heartbeat suddenly sounds louder and faster than the dance music. Kevin swallows, then swiftly surges forward, capturing my mouth with his. I can taste the chocolate on his tongue. I pull him closer still, so feral in my need for him I forget where we are and don't give any thought to the boundaries I've been insisting on.

The sound of a throat clearing breaks through my haze, and I pull back, blinking. I turn to see Dan, smirking at us in his groomsman's suit. My face heats, and I dart my eyes over to Kevin. He's laughing.

"Nice timing, Dan."

Dan holds up his hands. "Hey, I was just sent over here to tell Ramona that Katie needs her."

My face is still burning when I jump up. "Yep. Okay." My voice is hoarse, so I clear my throat. "On my way."

Kevin tugs my hand as I walk away, so I turn to look at him. His eyes are hooded, and a lazy smile plays at his lips. "Hurry back, baby."

All the heat from my face drains into my chest. My heart feels so full it could burst.

This night has been perfect. This whole week has been perfect. Which tells me it's about time for something to go terribly wrong.

Chapter Nineteen

I didn't know it was possible to feel exhausted and wired at the same time, but that's where I am when Kevin and I finally get home after Katie's wedding. We flop onto the couch, both too tired to change out of our formal clothes, and also not nearly ready to go to bed.

I rest my head against Kevin's shoulder, and he kisses the top of my head. After a few minutes, I find I'm not all that wired after all and begin to doze off.

When I realize it, I sit up. "Ready for bed?"

"Wait." Kevin darts into my bedroom, returning with an envelope in his hands, grinning. "I have something for you. It's your Christmas present. I wanted to wait until after the wedding to give it to you."

I scrunch my shoulders up to my ears. "Ooh, a present?" I hold out my hands and wiggle my fingers. "Gimme."

He chuckles and sits next to me on the couch, handing me the envelope. I carefully unstick the top flap and slide a folded piece of paper out. I open the paper and read.

"It's ... tickets to the Biltmore?"

Kevin bobs his head. "Yeah, for the second Saturday in January, while you're in Asheville. I know you were looking forward to it back in September and didn't get to go. I thought we could go together."

"Oh, I love it! Thank you, Kev." I wrap my arms around his torso and squeeze. He hugs me back, talking into my hair.

"It's a shame they'll have already taken down the Christmas decorations, though. The Biltmore at Christmas is something to see."

I smile and sigh. "It is on my bucket list."

Kevin's eyes light up. "I know! I'll take you next Christmas."

That stops me cold. I pull out of the embrace, leaning back and away from him. "Next Christmas?"

Future plans a whole year away. Will we still be doing this long-distance thing a year from now? What is the end game here with him in North Carolina and me in Georgia?

Kevin's eyebrows furrow. "Yeah. Why?"

I hesitate and then blurt, "Will we still be together next Christmas?"

For a second, I see a flash of hurt on Kevin's face. He squares his shoulders, taking my left hand and wrapping it up in both of his.

"My hope is we'll spend all our Christmases together. I want to spend every day, every minute with you, forever."

My nose stings as I blink back tears. I knew it. I knew this would blow up in our faces. If I thought I was heartbroken the first time I lost Kevin, it'll be nothing compared to how I'll feel this time.

I try to retreat, pull back on my feelings and convince myself, and Kevin, too, that we're not as serious as all that.

I pull my hand back and look at my lap while I speak. "Maybe ... maybe this whole thing has just been a bad case of summer camp love syndrome?"

Kevin's shoulders fall. "Of ... what?"

"Did you ever go to summer sleepaway camp?"

Kevin nods his head, so I continue.

"You know how at summer camp, relationships feel more intense? You form bonds with bunkmates and camp boyfriends, and they're so consuming. So extreme. But they only exist in that place, while you're together at camp. You go home at the end of the summer, and your real life drowns out all those feelings until they're memories. Our time together in college, and especially the days we spent in Asheville after the storm, were so emotionally charged, maybe it made us feel like this thing between us was more than it is."

"You don't believe that. Do you? Where is this coming from?"

The pain in his eyes, the confusion in his voice, don't stop me from lying through my teeth. If anything, it's the fact that the intensity of what I feel for Kevin is growing, not fading, that's causing problems. Because what's the endgame? Location will always be an insurmountable challenge. And I'll be left heartbroken again but worse.

I shrug.

Kevin's hands are on me now, rubbing my arms. Cupping my face. It's too much, and I know I won't be able to resist him. I never can. I pull away, my eyes locked on my feet. He tilts my chin up, forcing me to look him in the eye.

"Baby, if you're telling me honestly that's how you feel, I'll drive home now and leave you alone. But I..." He searches my face. "I don't think that's the case. It's definitely not how *I* feel. I made the mistake once of leaving you behind without telling you the truth about my feelings. I won't do it again." He takes a deep breath. "Ramona, I love you. I loved you in college. I was too young or stupid or scared to say it. I've never stopped loving you since. My normal life, though granted my life is not normal right now, hasn't made the intensity of my love for you fade. The opposite. I wake up every morning wishing you were next to me. I take care of the horses and remember you there with me. The thought of seeing you makes me embarrassingly giddy. I want to see you every day. Kiss you every day."

"But how? How, Kevin?" My restraint is gone. I know my voice is shrill, almost whiny, but I can't control it. He loves me. He loves me, but I can't see a path forward for us.

"Do you love me, Ramona?" I turn my head away. He holds my chin between his thumb and pointer finger, pulling my face back to his. I look into his eyes; the cornflower blue has transformed into a stormy gray. "Answer the question. Do you love me?"

"What difference does it make? Yes, I love you. It doesn't change geography. Love doesn't make it so we can snap our fingers, and our problems are solved, and we can somehow be together even though we're living two separate lives."

"I know! I know. We can figure something out. We can make it work." His voice is frantic, desperate. He shakes his head.

"Would you ... would you ever consider leaving Asheville and moving to Atlanta?" I ask. It's hypothetical; I'm not asking him to move, just testing the waters. His silence in response to the question says it all. "Oh."

"Ramona, I ... I don't know what to say here." He lifts his hand to his head as if preparing to flip his hat around. He realizes he's not wearing it and scrunches his fingers through his hair instead, making the strands stand on end. "That's a big ask. I have a family business to run in Asheville. My parents are counting on me. And I love the farm."

More than he loves me. It's maybe not what he meant to imply, but it's what I hear. He doesn't love me enough to leave the farm, or, apparently, to ask me to move to Asheville, which I might, if I knew he wanted me to.

"Where does that leave us then?"

Kevin smiles sadly. Cupping my chin in his hand, he says, "Here's lookin' at you, kid?"

Chapter Twenty

Kevin

♥

I'm in a rotten mood when I get back to the farm on New Year's Day. I snap at my dad when he innocently asks why I'm home already.

"Change in plans," I growl.

The next week, I swear I'm about to punch Davie in the face when he goads me about my general down-in-the-dumps attitude since New Year's.

"What, did your girlfriend break up with you?" he asks.

Instead of hitting my cousin, I ignore him and try to get back to my regularly scheduled life at the farm.

I don't *think* we're officially broken up, though Ramona and I did leave things in kind of a weird place. After our argument, or whatever you want to call it, I slept on the couch. Even though I was supposed to stay another night, Ramona asked for some space, so I drove home, my mind still reeling.

Now sitting at my kitchen table, clutching my coffee mug and working up the energy to go back outside into the cold to finish my chores, I think back on that conversation and still don't understand how it devolved so quickly. One minute I'm giving my girlfriend a thoughtful Christmas gift, and the next she's writing me off, then saying she loves me, and then asking me about moving to Atlanta.

We're still texting daily, but the messages feel strained. We've talked on the phone a couple of times; she was preoccupied, and the calls were short.

The weekend we planned for her to come to Asheville—the weekend I bought the Biltmore tickets for—is fast approaching, and I'm not sure she's going to come. I know I could ask her. Honestly, I'm afraid of what her answer will be.

Basically, I'm an idiot. I mean, am I really going to let this woman walk out of my life for a second time? I know I can't ask her to move here, not now. We have months and months of rebuilding left to do. It'll be hard even for those of us with Asheville in our bloodstreams.

I don't want to lose her. And, yeah, while my knee-jerk reaction was that I'm never leaving Asheville, never leaving this farm, when I think about being here without her, it feels wrong. Empty. So, if leaving the farm and moving to Atlanta is what it takes to be with the woman I love, I *am* willing to do that.

I've already talked to my dad about the potential of leaving Davie in charge. Davie won't be too keen on the idea. He doesn't like being in charge of anything. Dad and I agree he's capable of it, especially if Dad supervises him at first.

My next step is to call in a favor from a buddy of mine who runs a small horse farm down in Fayetteville, Georgia. See if he could use any help. It will undoubtedly be hired-hand work, at least at first, but it'll be something.

I'm distracted from this line of thought, and from making the phone call, by a knock on my cabin door. Thinking it's my dad or Davie trying to figure out where I disappeared to, I fling the door open.

It's not my dad, and it's not Davie. Instead, Ramona stands in front of me in jeans and a powder blue puffer jacket that swallows her whole.

"Ramona." I'm stunned. All I can think about is how desperately I want to wrap my arms around that marshmallow jacket and breathe her in. I've missed her so much. The emotional wall between us, not to mention the physical distance, has made me numb. Now, seeing her in front of me, my heart roars back to life, each nerve intent on making sure she's real.

"That's not my name," she says, one corner of her mouth tipped up in an unsure smile.

"What?" My brain is glitching. She's smiling. That has to be good. She's here, and she's smiling.

"Ramona's not my name anymore, remember? Not to you."

A smile starts to creep across my face. "Baby."

She beams and jumps into my arms without warning. I catch her under her knees. She nuzzles her face into my neck. She feels so good against me, despite the ridiculous coat.

"What are you doing here? What's going on?"

"I quit my job," she says, pulling her head back so I can hear her.

"You ... what?"

"I hated it anyway."

"Why?"

"It was boring. I didn't get to use half my skills. I never felt challenged or engaged—"

I laugh. "No, baby. Why did you quit?"

"To move to Asheville. I want to find a job here that's a better fit—"

Oh no. No, no, no. She can't make that kind of sacrifice.

"You're moving here? I can't let you do that. Asheville is in shambles right now, still, all these months later. What's here for someone like you?"

Ramona looks me directly in the eye. "You," she says simply. She scoffs. "Besides, it's not your decision. You don't get to 'let' me do anything."

My thoughts whirl, trying to put this all together. "Where will you live?"

"Your mom offered me a room in their house, at least until I can find something else."

I can't stop the grin on my face now. "Let me get this straight. You're moving to Asheville to be with me. And you're going to live right across this field right here in my parents' house."

"Yes." She slides down my body until she's standing on her own two feet again in front of me. She takes both my hands in hers and looks up at me earnestly.

"Kevin, I love you. I've been cautious, probably too cautious, about our relationship. I know what we have is a for-real, once-in-a-lifetime kind of love, and I don't want to lose you. I realize it wasn't fair of me to expect you to give up your life's work and your family's legacy to be with me in a city I don't have any real ties to, and where I'm not happy."

Still grinning, I shake my head.

"What?" she asks.

"Baby, I love you, too. I started loving you in college and never stopped, even when I convinced myself I'd moved on." I laugh. "Just now, before you knocked on the door, I was fixin' to call a buddy of mine in Fayetteville to see if he could use any help on his horse farm."

"Fayetteville, Georgia? Like the Fayetteville twenty miles from Atlanta?" Her eyes are wide with confusion.

I smile. "Yeah, Fayetteville, Georgia. I was going to turn the farm here over to Davie and move to Atlanta."

Ramona stares at me. "Why would you do that? Your life, your future, is here."

I shake my head. "There is no life or future for me without you in it. *You're* my life. *You're* my future."

I watch her eyes fill with tears. One escapes and trickles down her face. I reach up my hand and wipe it away. I smooth my thumb over her cheek, stroking gently. She wraps her arms around my neck; I bend, covering her mouth with mine. In that kiss, I feel all we meant to each other in college, the pain of losing touch, the joy in finding each other again, and the promise of forever.

Ramona rocks back on her heels, breaking our kiss, and regards me with a watery smile.

"Well then," she says. "I guess we have some decisions to make. Together."

I kiss her forehead. "That's all I ever want, from here on out."

Epilogue

♥

One Year Later

A light dusting of fresh, white snow covers the hills around the farm, and I think, like I do with each new season, maybe *this* is my favorite. I first experienced the now-familiar landscape in fall, when the leaves were starting to turn. I moved here in winter, when ice and frost glistened on the tree limbs and across the pasture. Spring brought its own wonders with wildflowers blooming in bright purple, pink, and yellow. Finally, the mountains in summer were so green they didn't seem real.

I've been in Asheville for a full year, building my marketing business for nonprofits. Early on, I took a lot of clients pro bono, especially local clients needing an extra boost to draw business after the devastation of the storm. Now, the work I've put in is starting to pay dividends. Each week I get a call or email from another organization who heard about the work I did for someone else and wants to hire me to help them, too. In another year or two, I may need to hire a second marketer to split some of the projects.

I stomp my feet to stay warm as I wait at the end of the driveway. Finally, a car turns the corner and pulls up in front of me.

Jonah climbs out of the driver's seat and grabs me in a big bear hug.

"Well, I got her here," he tells me with a wink.

I grin as Katie rounds the car, a grimace on her face. "Kicking and screaming," she says. "I hope you realize what it means about my love for you that I'm here at all. And in the freaking snow, too. With my luck, there will be some freak blizzard, and I'll be stuck here. Again."

I laugh. "It's for a good cause."

Her face softens, and she wraps her arms around me. "The best cause. You know I would never miss your wedding. Even if I have to come to the stupid mountains. Let it be known the sacrifices I make for you."

"You're a very good friend. Come on, let's get you settled. Beth, Dan, and the kids are staying in the infamous cottage, also known as your jail cell. I figured you two would be more comfortable in the big house."

"*Your* house, you mean?"

I grin. "Yes, after the wedding." Kent and Karen are moving into the cabin and giving Kevin and me the main house.

"Sounds like they hope you'll need the space for all the babies you're going to have."

I blush. "Anyway. Y'all are in the guest room. I'll show you where it is."

Katie grabs my shoulders, and I stop walking. Her face shines as she says, "Ramona, you're getting married tomorrow! Can you believe it?"

I can't stop the toothy smile that takes over my face, or my squeal as I answer her. "I can't believe it. When we were seniors in college, who would have guessed I'd marry Kevin? I didn't think I'd ever see him again."

When we started planning our wedding after Kevin proposed on my birthday this past September, we agreed getting married on the farm was the perfect choice for us. While Kevin would have been fine with something small and laid back, I insisted we go more upscale.

As my friends and I unload the car and carry their luggage into the house, workers are erecting a giant white tent in the pasture where they'll set up tables, chairs, and portable, outdoor heaters. The centerpieces of white flowers with lots of greenery are chilling in the basement until we set them up tomorrow. We're using only local companies, giving priority to those most affected by the storm when we could. Asheville still isn't what it was before the flooding, but we see new progress each day. And nothing can break the spirit of our unbeatable city.

The rest of the day is a blur of getting guests settled and directing vendors. I hardly see Kevin before the rehearsal that night, and at dinner, we're both so busy visiting with our guests, we don't have a moment alone together. Oh well. Tomorrow is the start of *lots* of moments alone together for the rest of our lives.

***

I'm pulled out of a restless sleep in my room in the big house by a soft kiss on my forehead and a familiar voice whispering, "Baby?"

I blink my eyes open to Kevin's face, his brow wrinkled.

"Kev?" I shoot up and fumble around for my phone. "What time is it?" The screen says five in the morning. "You're not supposed to see me on our wedding day! It's bad luck."

He chuckles, yet his face remains serious. "Baby, we've got bigger problems."

I rub my eyes. "What's going on?"

"Snowstorm. Come see."

He pulls me to the window in my room facing the pasture and mountains: white snow as far as the eye can see, with more still falling. The snow congregates in heaps on top of the wedding tent, the fabric sagging under the weight.

My wide eyes meet Kevin's. "That's a lot of snow."

"About six inches so far, with more on the way. They're calling for ten inches overall."

I groan. "What are we going to do?"

"I knew you'd be mad if I didn't tell you right away but we've got it handled. It's supposed to stop snowing by eleven. The crew wasn't planning to set up the tables and chairs until about noon anyway. We should have plenty of time to fix the tent and finish getting set up before the ceremony at four."

"Are you sure?"

He kisses my forehead. "Yes. I don't want you to worry."

He's right that when I woke up in the morning and saw the snow I would have been annoyed if he knew and didn't tell me. I like to know, even if there's nothing I can do.

"Okay," I say. "I trust you."

A relieved smile crosses his face. "Good. Now get some rest, and I'll take care of everything."

I stroke his cheek. "As long as I'm married to you before the day is over, I'll be happy, no matter the weather."

He kisses my lips softly. "Same."

A thought crosses my mind, and I scrunch my eyes closed with a sigh.

"What?"

I open my eyes and shake my head. "Katie is going to be so mad."

***

My dad holds my elbow as I start my walk down the aisle toward the man of my dreams.

As expected, the snow stopped by mid-morning, and the crew was able to fix the tent and get everything else set up before the ceremony. Beth tells me Kevin spent most of the day working right beside them until his mom dragged him away to shower and change about an hour ago. It's unfair how little time a man needs to get ready for his own wedding, especially compared to the hours I spent today being made-up and hair-dressed.

Time well spent now as my eyes lock with Kevin's, and I see his sharp intake of breath. He doesn't try to hide the tears in his eyes.

We stay focused on each other until I'm standing in front of him. My dad shakes his hand and gives me a hug before taking his seat in the front row next to my mom. I hand my bouquet to Beth and turn to face my fiancé.

Kevin takes my hands in his. "You're beautiful," he mouths. I beam at him. He looks handsome, too. He's wearing his gray tailored suit with a green tie the color of the mountains in summer.

Standing in front of the crowd, Kevin and I face each other. Despite the heaters in the tent, I shiver through the thin lace sleeves of my gown. Kevin catches my reaction and drops my hands. In one smooth motion, he removes his suit jacket and wraps it around my shoulders.

The audience collectively coos out an "Awww," and we all laugh.

Soon, the officiant asks us to recite the vows we've written. Kevin starts.

"Baby, standing here with you today is a dream come true. I can't believe you, the most amazing woman I've ever met, not only chose me but also chose this farm and this life I love too. I'm the luckiest man on Earth. And I'll spend the rest of our lives making sure you never regret your choice. I love you."

I blink back tears and take a moment to steady my shaking breath before my turn.

"Kevin, you were the first man I ever loved, even when we were both too young and afraid to admit that's what it was. There's no doubt in my mind now. I've never believed in fate, but how else can we explain how me and my friends ended up booking a vacation rental on your farm nine years after I never thought I'd never see you again? Whether fate or coincidence or dumb luck, I'm eternally grateful we found each other again. I promise to never let you go. I love you."

Kevin's shining gaze is latched onto my face, his smile broad as he lifts one of my hands to his lips and presses a gentle kiss to my fingers.

The officiant guides us through exchanging rings. When she pronounces us husband and wife, Kevin gets a mischievous glint in his eyes.

"You may now seal your vows with a kiss."

Grinning, Kevin wraps one arm behind my shoulders and pushes me back into a dip. He tilts his head toward mine and catches my lips in a searing kiss. It's far from the prim, sweet kiss we discussed being our first as a married couple, and I really don't mind. I loop my free arm around his neck and pull him closer.

Whistles and whoops from the audience break us apart, laughing. Kevin sets me back upright, murmuring in my ear, "To be continued."

The officiant is all smiles as she announces, "Beloved family and friends, I present to you Mr. and Mrs. Kevin and Ramona King!"

The crowd applauds, and Kevin thrusts our enjoined hands above our heads as if raised in victory.

We make our way up the aisle, the snow-covered mountains in the distance ahead. I tug Kevin's hand and, pulling him closer, say in his ear, "The start of forever."

He meets my eyes, his smile covering his whole face. "Baby, I'm so ready."

Acknowledgements

As I share in the Author's Note at the beginning of the book, *Second Chance in Asheville* was inspired by my own experiences being in Asheville, North Carolina when Hurricane (then downgraded to Tropical Storm) Helene came through.

As such, I want to thank our vacation rental hosts, Karen and Ramona (and Beth who communicated with us from another city via the app), for the inspiration their beautiful property provided.

Thank you for making sure we had food and bottled water and a power bank to charge our phones. Your city is beautiful, I'm just sorry we didn't get to see more of it.

Thank you to critique partners and beta readers Renee and Sharolyn, and especially Maddie, whose feedback was perfect. I'm grateful to Angelique and Gemma for reading over the horse parts to help me make sure they made sense. Thank you Ruth Shilling at RS Book Coaching and Editorial for your wonderful editorial eye – you helped me iron out a few wrinkles in the story that made everything work better.

Thank you Andy, Gabriel, and Ana. I know this writing hobby I've developed is keeping me busy. Your love and support are everything.

About the Author

Julie Milo spends most of her time reading and writing. When she's not reading and writing scholarly stuff for her day job, she's reading romance, nonfiction, and literary fiction for fun. She writes closed door/kisses only (also called "sweet") romantic comedies.

Julie was raised, but not born, in Florida where she started dictating stories to her parents before she even knew how to write. By kindergarten she was writing and illustrating picture books and subjecting her classmates to read alouds at school. While the illustrating did not stick (her drawing skills never evolved past about third grade), the writing did, and for most of her childhood, her answer to "What do you want to be when you grow up?" was "an author." Returning to writing decades later is a dream come true, and Julie is proud to finally be able to call herself an author.

Julie currently lives on the Gulf coast of Florida with her thoughtful husband, two amazing children, and two dogs (one delightful pit bull and one very energetic black lab). She loves dessert and hates cold weather.

You can learn more about Julie and her books at www.juliemilo .com.